STEELE

STEELE

•

Robert H. Redding

AVALON BOOKS
NEW YORK

© Copyright 2001 by Robert H. Redding
Library of Congress Catalog Card Number: 00-107017
ISBN 0-8034-9461-0
Published by Thomas Bouregy & Co., Inc.
160 Madison Avenue, New York, NY 10016

PRINTED IN THE UNITED STATES OF AMERICA
ON ACID-FREE PAPER
BY HADDON CRAFTSMEN, BLOOMSBURG, PENNSYLVANIA

In memory of Ernest Haycox,
writer of Westerns

Chapter One

When Steele left the gold mines of Idaho, he figured he was leaving as the toughest kind of man in the world. And he'd seen plenty. But when he hit Montana's north country, he changed his mind.

He had no sooner passed through the Rockies, and was pushing his jug-headed bronco, Fuzz, through summer-parched buffalo grass, when he was accosted. Five men rode up to him and stopped in a cloud of dust.

"You got any money?" one of them asked. He was a fat man, with a big nose and yellow teeth.

"No," said Steele.

"You just come from them mines in Idyho,

1

and you ain't got money. Hard t' believe, feller."

The fat-faced man glanced at his companions, and they all snickered. A great joke, they seemed to think.

The men were as unpleasant-looking a group as one could expect to find this side of Hell. He knew he was in real danger.

"We want your money," said the speaker.

For an answer, Steele drew his revolver and shot the man's hat off. It fluttered through the air like a wounded dove, then fell flat on the ground.

There was a stunned silence. Then the fat man said, "Hey, feller, we was peaceful—but not no more."

The five dove for their pistols.

"Don't," warned Steele, "or I'll shoot you all dead."

To emphasize his point, he aimed casually at a small rock. The .44 slug smashed it to bits. Shards whipped through the air like knives, and cut one of the horses. The animal leaped into the air and came down snorting.

"Sorry, horse," Steele apologized, "but I had to do that."

The gang snaked their collective hands back, leaving their firearms nested like alerted scorpions.

"Now," said Steele, "you-all just head out, and don't follow me. By the way, how did you know I came from 'Idyho'?"

"Everybody comes from your direction comes from there," was fat-face's sullen reply.

"And they all have money and gold?"

"Natchurly."

"Beat it," Steele ordered, wondering how many people from "Idyho" the group had murdered for gold. "And don't one of you try anything, unless you want lead in your brains, instead of mush."

The five retreated, but not without looking back, scowling and muttering. Steele faced them, astride Fuzz, his face planed into hard, smooth lines. He watched until the would-be robbers were dots on the prairie.

"Scum," he said to Fuzz, "just like the kind we left in Texas, boy."

Fuzz snorted in reply.

When he felt it was safe, Steele nudged the horse into action. Fuzz was a buckskin, with a peculiar knot of hair at the top of his mane, hence his name. He was a tough animal, and had carried Steele from Texas to the Idaho mines without much thought. His master fed him well, curried him often to soften his gnarled hair, and doctored his sores and aches, always speaking softly. He'd never heard Steele raise his voice in anger, not even after he'd thrown the man when a giant bee flew up a terrified nostril.

Steele had merely picked himself up, dusted himself off, boarded again, and said, "Well, now, feller, don't care much for bees myself."

Feeling safe again, Steele reached in a saddle bag and squeezed a fat poke. He smiled. The gold was the payoff for ten months of hard labor in the Gold King, a hard-rock mine. It was a pretentious handle for an operation that folded after a year, but the company did pay its men. Many did not, claiming bankruptcy. Steele was lucky.

After the mine closed, he drifted. He bought breakfast in Orofino, and supper in Lewiston. He worked his way north into Idaho's panhandle, looking for a job, and spent time in Kellog.

Everywhere he went, he met trouble. Men fought him, quarrelsome and mean. Some were after his poke; some fought because they had to let off steam. The big mines were closing. The gold rush days of Idaho were sliding down the sluice boxes, and there was no work. Most of the men were professional miners, and not knowing what to do next, they turned mean. Some left for the Black Hills of Dakota, where, it was said new strikes were being made. Only trouble with that was the Indians. There were fights and killings, the Indians defending one of the last good hunting grounds from the white man. Nevertheless, miners departed there to find out for themselves.

Steele didn't look on himself as a professional miner, even after his Gold King experience. He was a cattleman by trade, and had once owned a small spread in northern Texas. He became, by necessity, a member of a posse, who then cleaned out a pack of hard-nosed rustlers. That made him, in a sense, a lawman.

Whenever Steele thought of his lawman days, he frowned, and quickly tried to think of something else. He didn't like what he remembered.

Being a member of a posse was not a boy's game. It was a bloody, tragic series of incidents. After the rustlers were dead, or chased out of the country, Steele sold his ranch.

"I need some fresh air," he told friends.

"But it ain't like you to run off," his friends had objected. "We might need you again. You're the best shot we got."

"I'm going," Steele had insisted. "When the stink of blood is out of my nose, I'll come back. Maybe."

The past was slowly becoming something he could live with, but he was glad to be where he was now, in the clear Montana air, on the sturdy back of Fuzz. Next thing was to find work.

Or maybe, thought Steele, *we'll try the Black Hills, Fuzz. Mining pays good, and we might just as well get the big pay jobs, eh? Or find a mine of our own.*

However, thinking about a return, to the Black Hills and actually getting there were two different things. Steele didn't know the way from where he stood on his compass. He worked his way East slowly, inquiring about routes along the way. He tried to pick the shortest ones to save Fuzz's hoofs from too much knocking on the hard ground. Right now, he was following Montana's Milk River.

Every night he made camp early, and rose early, putting in a long day of traveling. As he traveled, he marveled at the complete flatness of the land. He could see for miles.

"Expect to see New York any day," he told his horse. "Rising right out of the plains."

The Rockies rose in back of him, an abrupt, snow-capped wall of stone and forests. Then there were the Great Plains. Mountains. Plains. There were no rolling hills, just a quick departure from one world, a world of great peaks and green trees, to a world of flat land, yellow and brown and hard.

One day Steele was grinding his way through a meal of hardtack and jerky, when six dots appeared on the horizon. Steele suspected the dots were people, and he was glad of it. He hadn't seen a soul in two days, and he knew he was getting close to the Big Sandy, his next river trail. But how could he be sure when he reached it? There were a number of streams cutting off from the Milk River. Would his goal be marked with a sign painted in red saying THIS IS THE BIG SANDY RIVER? Hardly.

The dots grew into half a dozen Indians. They were mounted bareback on rangy little mustangs. One of the Indians wore a blue Army jacket, a sergeant's. The Indians trotted their horses up to Steele warily. Their faces showed no emotion, and Steele didn't know if they were ready to befriend him or kill him. He tensed, his hand not far from his Colt.

The Indians studied him with bleak, dark eyes for a few moments, then pointed at his pistol.

"We want that gun," said one.

"You can't have it," Steele told him.

"Then we will take it," said the Indian.

They were armed, Steele noted, with two .45-70 single-shot rifles, and bows and arrows. From the sound of the Indian's voice, Steele knew that the group would indeed take his pistol. So he drew it and shot, first the two carbines. They flew away, badly damaged. The arrows came, and one grazed Steele's thigh.

Another thunked into Fuzz's saddle, and another stung his arm. Steele quickly shot the bows from the hands of the others, splintering the wood.

There was rage and confusion, and Steele quickly reloaded while the Indians circled on their ponies. They were unarmed now except for knives. They drew these, prepared to charge. Steele leveled his .44.

"I don't know how much English you understand," he told his dark-skinned adversaries, "but you do understand pure Colt, right?"

The six halted, and the Indian speaker stared at the white man with the steady pistol. His eyes narrowed like those of an angered prairie wolf.

"We know English," he said. "We learned on *white* reservations." He spoke with contempt. "You," he went on, "beat us, yet we are more than you. But you did not kill us. Why?"

"I have no wish to kill. I have had enough killing."

"Enough?"

"It is a story that is my own."

The Indian nodded, then spoke. "A man's life

is his secret." He paused before continuing. "I am Two Dogs, one of the Cheyenne war chiefs. I do not like whites, and I will tell you this— there will be a big war soon. We need white man's guns. You made two of our rifles no good. You will pay."

"Don't ever come near me again," said Steele. "Next time I will not shoot your weapons."

Two Dogs was a lean man, tall. The muscles of his bared stomach rippled, and armbands pressed tight against his long muscles. He raised a hand, and surprised Steele with an Army salute, then wheeled his pony and trotted off. The others followed.

Steele watched, and was surprised again to hear laughter. It came from Two Dogs, and was derisive. He was gesturing, and made clear he was teasing the others. They had been beaten by one lone man, and their weapons destroyed. The war chief's men were being disciplined in the Indian way—by mockery. It was, thought Steele, as good a way as any.

As with the would-be robbers, Steele watched until the Indians were dots, then vanished in a wash of heat waves. Then he turned his attention to his wounds. He went to the river and bathed them. They were bloody, but not serious. He'd had worse. They would bring discomfort, but would heal without infection if kept clean.

Fuzz had calmed in the meantime, and was drinking with gusto from the river. His soft nose was stuck deep, and he sucked in huge droughts of the refreshing liquid. Steele dumped the old water from his canteen, and refilled it. He glanced warily downstream. The Big Sandy had to be near.

He was weary, but moved with alert caution. There could be more Indians around, probably unfriendly. He wondered about the "big war" Two Dogs spoke of. He knew of the trouble between whites and Indians, but he couldn't define "big war." The words could mean anything from a farmhouse raid to the massacre of some wagon train travelers. If the war was really big, he would hear of it. If it involved only a few, the news would probably not reach him.

Right now, the safety of his own life, and that of Fuzz, were in question. An ambush bullet could quickly end his plans for the Black Hills and home. He opened his ears to the sounds of nature, and listened for a difference. The song of the meadowlark was natural. Ducks quacking on the river were natural. Even the whispers of the constant breeze were expected and right, but Steele knew the sound of a sharp click would not be natural. The click could be a horse's hoof striking a rock, or the backward thrust of a rifle's hammer. A snapping twig could mean the approach of an elk, perhaps, or a horse—or a man on foot.

As flat as the country was, Steele was certain that the Indians—the Cheyenne or Sioux or whatever tribe—could always find ways to remain unseen. There were dry river beds with high banks, the steep draws, tall buffalo grass. As he rode, Steele felt the muscles in the small of his back tighten. He had the unpleasant sensation of being watched, but he had no way to know for sure.

After a while he reached the Big Sandy. He was sure of the river, because, for one thing, it was larger than the other offshoots of the Milk. It also headed almost directly south, and, as a final clue, there were tracks, a sort of trail. If this wasn't the Sandy, at least the trail led someplace, and he'd find out.

He rode for several hours, and came to a town so small that the place was more like a camp of clapboard lumber sheds and a single dusty street. It began abruptly and ended as abruptly, hunched up like a buffalo's hump. Steele guided Fuzz to a hostelry, and left him with an order to feed him well.

He signed for a room at the only hotel, and took a hot bath. He itched from alkali dust, and his wounds throbbed. He dressed in his cleanest clothing afterward, and and went to a restaurant for some dinner. In the restaurant, he saw several cowboys pestering a girl sitting alone. She was pale, but pretty. She was not a flirty dance hall girl, Steele realized, noticing how she sat primly in heavy riding clothes, trying to ignore the cowboys.

"Do you know her?" Steele asked the men.

"What's it to you?" one replied, and Steele detected a Texas accent.

"I don't think she knows you. I think she wants to be left alone."

"Keep outta this," said another. "We's just havin' a little fun."

"Beat it," said Steele.

The girl looked at him.

"I think," you'd better be the one to beat it," said another cowboy.

There were scowls on the faces of the teasing punchers now. There were four of them, and their daily work, one of the most dangerous occupations in the world, had knocked fear out of them.

"What's next?" Steele asked.

They came at him in a flood of flailing fists. He staggered back, but drew his fists and struck back. He was strong. He used to lift 200-pound kegs of spikes over his head, while loading freight wagons in Idaho. He also knew how to fight. He'd had plenty of experience in Texas—too much experience, but experience was just that, and it led to mastery of certain situations as it did now.

He fought the cowboys to the door, and they spilled out, an avalanche of human flesh. Boots, arms, bodies and legs whirled into the street, a great tangle. After they were out,

Steele slammed the restaurant door shut, then stood on the porch.

The enemy dusted itself off, and stood in the street getting ready for another charge, when one suddenly asked, "Say, judgin' by your talk, feller—ain't you from Texas?"

"That I am."

"Huh, thought so. Nobody but a Texican can fight like that."

"Be danged," muttered another of the quartet, "we been fighting our own."

"Hey," put in another man, "we just havin' fun. Meant no harm to the pretty lady."

"Scaring her half to death is fun?" Steele was scornful. "You want a girl? Go over to a saloon, you bums."

There was a moment of hesitation, and Steele knew that Texas pride was on the rise. Could they allow one man to beat four of them?

Finally, one drawled, "Since you're from the old country, feller, we'll let the matter drop. We're GTT, anyway. Time t' git."

"GTT?" Steele was curious about the term.

"Goin' to Texas, man," was the reply, and the four walked out of his life.

Steele returned to the restaurant. The girl was gone.

"Well looky that," he muttered. "This sure is unfriendly country. I get in three fights, and the last one is to rescue a fair lady, and the fair lady disappears on me. She could've at least said, 'Thank you, sir,' before the fare-thee-wells."

He sat down and ordered steak and eggs from a nervous waiter, and pretty soon was his old self again. Life, he thought, was funny.

Chapter Two

Before leaving town, Steele looked again for the girl, but she was gone.

That's gratitude, he thought. *On the other hand, what would a lady like that want with the likes of me?*

He took stock. His clothing consisted of jeans, a blue cotton shirt, a heavy woolen jacket, a Stetson, which he had creased lengthwise down the middle, and—his only fancy garb—a pair of San Antonio hand-crafted boots with tooled leather. He carried a .44 Colt, a single-action revolver, in a shiny black holster, and extra cartridges in some belt loops. Not many cartridges, because he didn't like the weight. Most of his extra shells were in the saddle bags.

No, he admitted, *I am no stage idol. If I were a girl I wouldn't look twice even if I did rescue her from Texas foolery.*

He dismissed the young lady from his mind and headed toward Deadwood. Following the river routes through Missouri, Yellowstone, and Big Horn, Steele made it to his goal in Dakota Territory. It was late September.

Deadwood was a busy place. The town was the largest supply depot for miners in the Black Hills. Wagons groaned through the dusty streets. Riders galloped in a frenzy, men shouted, women shrieked, and stores sagged with abundant goods. There was enough gold in the Black Hills to make everybody rich, so the talk went. But there was a splinter in the dream—the Indians claimed the ground. It was given to them in a treaty signed in '68, by gar. So much for treaties. What was on top of the ground might be theirs, but what was under it belonged to everybody. Whoever got that gold first was the rightful owner. Let the blamed Injuns take their chances.

There had been fights, Steele learned.

"I was in the Peck bunch," one old-timer informed him. "Man, he was just inside the drainage of the Powder River, when them redskins hit us. They killed everyone except me and one other. We hid out in the river all day, and they took all our goods." The old-timer, with an arrow wound through his hand, shook his head. "I lost everything except my life." He grinned. "And I'm goin' back with what's left of it."

The Indians attacked small parties looking for gold, and let the big ones alone. Good strategy, Steele reckoned. Be sure of your game. The U.S. Army, tried keeping the miners out of the Black Hills, thus honoring the '68 treaty, but they were persistent. Gold was a powerful lure. Hostilities increased, and there were many attacks.

"It isn't legal," Steele pointed out to a promoter named Red Clark. "Whites, the way I see it, have no right being here."

"The Army don't really care any more," Clark said. He was a large, florid man. He reminded Steele of a cow freshly skinned. "The Army and the Injuns are negotiating in Washington right now, and nobody knows what's going to happen."

"So?"

"So the Army don't know which way to turn. The thing's in the air. Oh, they still send men into them hills and kick prospectors out, but there's too many whites. Can't catch 'em all."

"We take you where it's safe," said a man with Clark.

Steele looked the man over closely. His name was Pat Lawrence, and Steele didn't like him. Could have been the way the man dressed, all in black, including his flat, broad-brimmed hat. Even his gauntlets were black, but there was contrast. His pistol sported ivory grips, and the weapon was nickel-plated. Around the man's neck was a silk kerchief of many colors, a strange contrast to the somber black of his clothes. He had a dark, drooping handlebar mustache, and his hair was long, flowing over his shoulders.

Pat Lawrence was a *frontiersman*.

Steele detested the type. They were show-men, mostly, putting on an act, making the most of their "westerness." The dashing dress and good-looks impressed newcomers. Pat Lawrence could have been a stage actor with his finely chiseled features. Even his actions were theatrical, large and expansive. Steele didn't like him, but he was also a little jealous. Maybe if he looked like Pat Lawrence that pretty girl would have given him at least a polite thank you. Lawrence cut a striking figure.

"By the way," Lawrence said pleasantly, "never caught your name."

"Never gave it."

Lawrence's eyes flickered at the turndown, but Clark laughed nervously, a husky rasp, and said, "Oh, well, lots of no-names in this country, right, Pat?"

The man in black gauntlets smiled without humor, and nodded. "Sure enough, but we got to have a handle if you join our party." His voice was still pleasant, and, Steele noted, he was well-spoken, proper. He seemed to be well-known, and was greeted by many as they passed.

"Haven't made up my mind," Steele told him. "When you leaving?"

"We go to Candy Mountain in ten days," Clark responded.

"I'll let you know in nine days."

"The group is limited to thirty people."

"Make it thirty-one."

Clark and Lawrence glanced at each other, and then Clark nodded. "We'll see."

"Fine." Steele had no doubt he could become a member, but he had a question. "Why ten days' delay? Winter's coming."

"We have business," Lawrence said.

"Don't worry, we'll get you to the mining grounds before freezeup," added Clark in his warm-butter voice.

"I'll bet you will."

"See you in ten—ah, *nine* days?" asked Clark.

"Maybe."

The two left with perfunctory farewells, and hurried to their office over a saloon.

"He's a danger," said Lawrence.

Clark nodded. "That he is. Still, if he's got a thousand or two, we might as well have it."

"And I do like that horse of his."

"We've dealt with tougher customers than no-name."

Lawrence grinned, revealing startling white teeth. "All right. He's in—but he's out first trip."

"Agreed."

The two got on their horses and left town. They rode steadily for three days, stopping only to eat and sleep. On the third day, they joined a band of Indians, under the leadership of Two Dogs.

Clark got straight to the point.

"They still there?" he asked Two Dogs.

Two Dogs nodded. His dark eyes were unreadable, and Clark didn't try. They had already agreed on what was to be done and Clark didn't care what the Cheyenne war chief thought.

The whites and Indians continued on together for half a day more through the forested hill country. They drove their horses as much as possible in the shadowed cool places. In the late afternoon, Clark, who was leading, raised his hand, a signal to halt.

"We'll attack on foot," he said. He motioned to Lawrence and Two Dogs. "Let's have a look first. The rest of you can wait here."

The three crept through the trees, and stood atop a small hill. In the hollow beyond were a number of wagons. The sound of voices drifted in the air—children, women, men.

"They don't even have a guard posted," observed Clark happily.

"Easterners don't know enough," Lawrence replied. "One of the reasons this is so easy."

He turned to Two Dogs. "They think we went for supplies." He rubbed his hands together. "I'm a good actor."

Clark snickered. "Better peel that mustache off before we begin."

Lawrence tugged an end of his flowing lip hair, and it came off, leaving his face bare. He tucked it carefully in a pocket, then both he and Clark stripped down to what appeared to be Indian loincloths.

Two Dogs watched impassively. At a nod from Clark, he pursed his lips and imitated a meadowlark perfectly. His band appeared on silent, moccasined feet. Where did they come from?

"When I say, 'Go,' we hit," Clark instructed, and Two Dogs nodded.

Clark checked his pistol, then shouted, "Go!"

The entire band charged, firing rifles, pistols, bows and arrows into the unsuspecting group. There followed a savage fifteen minutes of killing, a horrible blasphemy of a massacre. Women were tomahawked, men stabbed, children clubbed. There were fearful cries of, "Why?" "Who are you?" "What's happening here?" "Run!"

The last shrieked sentence rang out too late, for nobody could run. They were cut off from escape, and every man, woman, and child was slain.

During the massacre, Two Dogs remained aside. He did not join his braves or the two white men. He was not after the scalps of children, or more jackets of men. He was after weapons. He needed many of the white man's firearms and ammunition for the inevitable war that would soon erupt. Those weapons meant freedom for his people, freedom from white man domination—but he did not take part in the massacre. He stood aside, until all was silent, then rode forward.

Clark and Lawrence, bloody and triumphant,

nodded at a stack of rifles, pistols, and ammunition.

"You got what you wanted, chief?"

Two Dogs nodded, then spoke quickly to his men. Sullenly, they threw down the items of loot they had taken from the slain—the men's jackets, boots, women's bonnets.

"We want nothing that will show we have been here," said Two Dogs curtly.

"But the whites will suspect Indians, anyway," Clark said. "Might as well make the most of it."

"That is true, but we will take nothing, except what we bargained for, the weapons." He spat on the ground. "You can have all the rest."

He motioned to his braves, who gathered the weapons and ammunition.

"We will do this again?" he asked Clark.

"Soon," Two Dogs replied.

"Very soon," echoed Lawrence. "We will tell you where and when."

Two Dogs nodded. He motioned to his people, and they left. They found their horses, strapped the new weapons to horses brought along for this purpose, and left without a look

back, but Two Dogs was thinking. If his face
and eyes showed little, his mind worked furi-
ously. He hated Clark and Lawrence. They
were traitors to their own kind so they could
make money. But he worked with them because they could give him what he needed—
weapons. He could trade for some guns, but
more were needed—more, maybe, than he
could ever get.

But, as he and his band headed for their village, he thought of the two whites with great
distaste, for honor was his highest priority.
That lone man on the river, who fought him
and five others, there was an honorable man!

At the scene of the massacre, Clark and
Lawrence got the wagons ready to roll, ignor-
ing the bodies of the innocent civilians. In the
wagons was the merchandise Clark had sold to
the slain people a few weeks earlier. He now
had the supplies back—plus a nice profit from
the money they originally paid him.

The two set out for Deadwood with their
goods.

"A nice few weeks' work, Lawrence," declared
Clark gleefully. "A couple more of these, and
we'll be on easy street."

Lawrence smiled, and his false mustache, which he had replaced, seemed to do its own jig of contentment.

"I love my work," he said, then added seriously, "but we have to be careful. That no-name fellow back in town is from Texas, according to his drawl. No doubt about that."

"You can handle him," Clark responded. "If he goes on the Candy Mountain trip and gives you any trouble, just kill him."

"That I will do."

Chapter Three

"How much is it going to cost me?" Steele asked.

"A thousand," Red Clark said.

"That is a bunch of money," said Steele.

"Remember, we furnish everything—grub, tools, even wagons, if you need one. And we guide you right to Candy Mountain."

"Candy Mountain?"

"Man," Clark's voice dropped, "that's the richest spot in the Blacks. Pat was there last month, and he saw it. Those who got claims are keeping mum. They don't want a rush."

"We can guarantee you'll make your thousand back," said Lawrence, "but I'll do more.

I'll personally return your money five to one, if you don't hit it rich."

"Sounds too good to be true," Steele said. He knew about mining from his time in Idaho. Most "strikes" petered out quickly.

The man in black stiffened, and his eyes flashed. Then he laughed.

"Well, I appreciate your caution, stranger. I'm sure you don't doubt my word?"

"Oh, no," Steele replied with the same false warmness that Lawrence delivered to him. "Like you say, I'm a stranger here, and don't know much."

Their conversation was interrupted by several men, all intent on joining the Candy Mountain party. Conversation drifted away from Steele, and he left, still undecided. He could feel Lawrence's hostile eyes following him, but Steele had met worse. Pat Lawrence, with his fancy, ivory-handled, nickel-plated six-shooter, didn't bother him in the least.

He retrieved Fuzz from the stable, and went for a ride up the crowded street. It was pure bedlam. There were whites, Indians, boys, girls, dogs, wagons, horses, donkeys and oxen, all milling together, talking, shouting, laughing, and swearing. Dust rose in a thick cloud, but nobody seemed to mind—the prospect of finding gold soothed all discomforts. Piano and banjo music from the bars added to the lively atmosphere, and every now and then, some liquored-up cowboy let loose with his .45. It was a wild and free town, and if there was a lawman around, he remained discreetly low-key.

Steele was about to leave town for the clear air beyond, when he saw the girl from the other night at the Saloon. She was sitting on a box beside a dozen freighting wagons in a string, with people busy loading on them. Steele rode over to the girl, and tipped his hat.

"How do you do?" he asked.

She glanced up at him. She was very pretty, Steele thought, with dark hair, gray eyes, a firm chin, and high color in her cheeks. She was even beautiful, he realized.

"Do I know you?" she inquired crisply.

"Sort of." Steele was amused. "Do you remember those Texicans?"

The gray eyes narrowed, and suddenly a warm smile lit her face.

"Of course! I never did thank you for that."

"That's why I'm here," Steele teased.

The high color in the girl's cheeks increased. "I apologize for running off like that. I'm not one to run from danger—but I didn't know what to expect, not even from my rescuer."

"I can understand that, Miss." At least, Steele hoped she was a Miss. Steele took a guess. "You're from the East?"

"Boston."

"You're a long way from home."

"My father has wanderlust. He wants to see some of the country, before he dies."

"Is he ill?"

"No!" The girl laughed, and Steele liked the sound. "He's just that way. He was a professor of literature for thirty years, and, suddenly, he just said, 'Let's go West!' So here we are."

"Had enough of teaching, did he?"

"I think that's part of it."

The conversation lagged, but Steele wanted to keep talking. He had known women in his life, but there was something special about this girl that drew him to her. He wanted to know her better.

"These wagons," he said. "Are you with them?"

"Yes."

"And?"

"Well, it's supposed to be a secret, but I guess I can confide in a man who saved me from much embarrassment. We are going to Candy Mountain."

Steele suddenly felt a chill. "Are you being equipped by a pair named Red Clark and Pat Lawrence?"

"Why, yes. In fact, Mr. Lawrence is going to guide us. Do you know them?"

"We've met."

"Mr. Lawrence seems so capable. I'm so excited!"

"I hear the Indians are protesting whites being in the Black Hills," Steele said.

"Oh, Mr. Clark assured us it was safe. Mr. Lawrence did, too."

"I imagine they would," Steele responded dryly.

"What was that?"

"Nothing. Just thinking out loud."

"My father and I feel quite secure. Mr. Clark

sold us all of our supplies for the journey, and I'm sure he wouldn't be sending us into trouble."

"I'm glad you and your father are so certain."

"Aren't you?"

"Oh, yes," Steele lied, not mentioning the recent massacre of whites in the Hills. He didn't want to scare her. "I'm sure those two know just what they are doing." He hesitated. "I'm called Steele.

The girl, whose face had clouded under Steele's doubtful tones, brightened. "I'm Elizabeth White.

Steele tipped his hat once more. "Until we meet again, Miss White."

"Yes . . . goodbye."

He left her, glancing back once to see a lone figure of a young woman watching him. She seemed vulnerable standing there, completely unaware that the country she lived in now was not like Boston. Boston, he'd heard, had its own toughs, but he doubted if any of them could match Indians on the warpath, or scamps like Clark and Lawrence. Steele had nothing concrete on which to base his opinion of the two whites—just instinct. But that instinct made up his mind for him. He sought out Red Clark, and forked over a thousand.

"You won't regret it," Clark cried happily. "And you are just in time—you are, as you requested, number thirty-one in our little group. The books are closed on the Candy Mountain expedition."

"When do we leave?"

"Tomorrow at dawn." Clark glanced at the bright blue sky. There was a chill in the air. "Winter's coming, and we have to get our people settled."

Steele was satisfied. He wanted to make some money, yes, and if Clark and Lawrence spoke even a quarter of the truth, he might. But he also wanted to see more of a young woman named Elizabeth White—and now he would.

The caravan of wagons left under the leadership of Lawrence. Clark remained in Deadwood to prepare more wagon trains. Thirty-one men and women headed into the starchy hills.

By the end of the first day, Steele realized the going would be slow. It was the end of September, and cold came early to the northern

Plains they were traveling. Could the party reach its destination, and have time to prospect the gold before freezeup?

"Hopefully," said Lawrence, when Steele put the question to him that night. "Yes, I think we will, but chances are we will have to winter there."

"According to your offer, I'd have plenty of gold in a few weeks—months at most," Steele reminded the train leader.

"Oh, I still hold to that," was Lawrence's smooth answer, "But you must know I can't guarantee a real hit at first."

Steele's anger was swift. "You exaggerate, Lawrence."

"You mean I'm a liar?"

"Call it what you want—but your promises are pretty vague."

Lawrence didn't mince words. "You can quit right now, fella—"

"Steele . . ."

"Steele. You can have your thousand back soon as you see Clark in Deadwood."

"I'm staying."

"Then don't question me. I don't like it."

"I'll question you as often as I please—and the answers better be better than the one I just got."

Lawrence tensed. He faced Steele squarely. The two were at the verge of a showdown when someone called for Lawrence. The two men didn't flinch, but the caller persisted. Lawrence suddenly relaxed.

"Don't worry," he said softly. "All will be well." He turned and left.

Steele smelled a rat—a big one. His instinct that something was wrong felt stronger. Lawrence's answers *were* vague. Was this some sort of a game? Were Lawrence and Clark con men? Was the wagon train being led into nowhere for some reason? The idea was unsettling, and it wouldn't leave. He was beginning to think there might be real danger from Lawrence, but he said nothing to anybody about it. He only had suspicions—no evidence. Now the caravan was on its way, money had been paid—there was no turning back.

In the evening, Steele visited the campfire of Elizabeth White and her father, Ezra. Ezra was a soft-spoken, white-haired man, a bit heavy around the middle. He never complained, and seemed to enjoy, to relish even, the hardships of wagon travel. He and his daughter had traveled all the way from St. Louis by wagons, so they were not new to the method. He performed his share of camp duties such as watering stock, gathering wood, and standing watch, and Steele took a liking to the older man. But the retired college professor puzzled him.

"This isn't your kind of life," Steele said to him. "Why do it?"

"Ever hear of Ralph Waldo Emerson?" Ezra asked.

"Can't say I have. Is he an actor?"

Ezra White laughed. "No, he's an American writer, a philosopher. One of the things he advocates for is to live life to the fullest. To put it in four simple words: do your own thing."

"Sounds reasonable."

"Exactly." Ezra White heaved a slow sigh. "I have done that partly by spending my working years in academia, but I don't feel complete yet."

"What do you mean?"

"I mean I haven't lived to the fullest that I

can. Up here," he tapped his head, "maybe, but here," he indicated his body, "I have not. I want to use all of me before I die."

"You want to do your own thing completely?"

"Exactly." The white-haired professor paused, then asked, "You are a man of the outdoors. You've been around this western outland. What do you think of what I've just told you? Do you think I'm some sort of a crazy?"

Steele shook his head. "We all live our lives according to what we are. A man does what he does, and that's the way it is. Why did you ask?"

Elizabeth came into the conversation. "His colleagues told him he was crazy for doing this." Her eyes sparkled with fire. "I think they were jealous. They don't have the courage to leave the safe and secure. *My* father did."

"You have a champion in your daughter," Steele said. "Let me tell you something . . ."

"What?" The older man was interested.

"I had a nice little spread in Texas. I am a good cattleman. Well, certain things happened, and I wanted a change—so I made it. Sold out and left. People down south thought I was foolish, but I feel good about what I've done. What about you?"

White nodded. "Never been more content."

"Then that's good enough, isn't it?"

"Yes, of course." White glanced at his daughter, with a glint in his eye. "Now there's a man for you, Liz. He's got some good ideas about life."

"Father!"

Elizabeth blushed. So did Steele.

White laughed, delighted. "Well, now, don't take it too hard, either of you. Still," he grew serious, "both of you could do worse."

As the nights multiplied, Pat Lawrence sometimes joined the firelight. He was ingratiating to the Whites, spoke courteously, and was always a gentlemen. In his black clothing, dashing hat, and white-handled pistol, he cut a fine figure. The drooping mustache didn't hurt, either, nor his handsome face. He always maintained the air of a frontiersman, a larger-than-life man of the West, the romantic myth that always held easterners spellbound. Steele, with jealous eyes, saw that Elizabeth was taken with him. That grated him, and subsequently he was more critical of daily matters.

"Sure slow going," he said to Lawrence one evening at the White's campfire.

"Can't hurry the oxen. They travel at one pace."

"I think there were places you could have cut a few miles off the trail."

Lawrence's face hardened. "You want to lead this train, fellow?"

"Oh, I'm sure Mr. Lawrence is capable," Elizabeth interrupted, sensing trouble.

"Yes," agreed Steele sarcastically, "I'm sure he is."

Lawrence rose. He bowed slightly to Elizabeth and her father. "I'd better be going," he said. "Got to visit other wagons to see if anything is needed."

"Very generous of you," said Elizabeth.

"Not at all. It's my job."

He turned an evil eye on Steele, and left.

"Weren't you unnecessarily hard on him?" Elizabeth said to Steele.

"He's a pompous ass."

"The jealous heart knows not courtesy," White put in slyly.

Steele flushed, embarrassed. "I'm jealous of nobody."

Ezra laughed. "All right, have it your way—for now."

"Your father seems to be reading something into me that isn't there," Steele said to Elizabeth.

"He's a very smart man, Steele."

"Why would I be jealous of that blowhard?"

"You mean that handsome cavalier of the frontier?"

"He's a blowhard," Steele repeated.

"I've never heard him blow hard. In fact, I think he's a great asset to our group."

Steele didn't want to argue about Lawrence. For one thing, he realized the more he attacked Lawrence, the more the girl would defend him. It was a losing battle.

"I suppose, you are right," he said quietly. "I shouldn't be so hard on that postcard."

Ezra laughed out loud, but Elizabeth did not. She turned away angrily, and Steele, seeing he had lost after all, bid them both good night.

Lawrence was waiting for him in the shadows behind the wagons. "Leave. There's not enough room for us both."

"No," Steele replied, "I stay."

Lawrence nodded. "I thought you'd say that, so I'll create an accident for you."

Steele saw Lawrence's gun hand move, but he was faster. He wasn't wearing his own firearm, so he leaped forward and clamped a hand around Lawrence's wrist, giving it a quick, strong flip. The gun clattered to the ground.

"You want to fight?" Steele held up a knotted set of knuckles. "We'll do it with these."

Lawrence tumbled back, regained his balance, and squared off with Steele.

Both were large-framed men, hardened by the life they lived in the wilderness. Both had had their share of human conflict as well. They bore scars. They were experienced in survival.

They fought silently, each man concentrating on the shadow before him. The remarkable thing Steele noticed, even then, was nobody in the train heard them. The fight was silent, but they did make noises—scuffings, fists on flesh, a gun thudding on the ground, noises that should have caught attention. He knew the answer: nobody in the train paid attention. All were strangers in a strange land, greenhorns. Noises in the shadows would hold no intimations of danger. Noises, for them, would be a horse grazing, a squirrel scampering, and a night bird.

Certainly, there was no danger in the noises heard.

The two men were about equal in weight and length of arm, so their swings—not well-placed in the dark—equaled the other's. But, they left their marks. Steele knew his nose was bloody, and his eyes were sore; there was a cut on his chin, and he knew Lawrence suffered injuries. The face was the most visible.

After the two realized that neither was going to win, they dropped their fists. Steele retrieved Lawrence's pistol. He unloaded it, and handed the weapon back.

"A Smith and Wesson," he noted. "Pretty good gun."

"Good enough."

"If so, why didn't you shoot me in the back? I'm sure you know how."

"I would have," Lawrence hissed, "but I don't want Indians hearing shots at night."

"Indians?"

"You know they've been trailing us for days."

"Yes," Steele replied. "But what difference would it make if they heard a night shot?" Steele bore down on Lawrence. "Wouldn't be some kind of signal, would it?"

Lawrence ignored the question. "Keep away from her," he growled.

"Her?" Steele asked.

"Don't play the fool with me, mister."

"I'll see her all she can stand of me." Steele felt Lawrence's hot eyes glaring at him in the gloom.

"Just keep away," Lawrence warned again, and then strode off toward his own camp.

Steele returned to his fire, heated water, and washed the blood from his face. All the while he wondered if Lawrence really thought he had a chance with Elizabeth. Steele already knew the answer, and he didn't like it. Elizabeth didn't seem to dislike the man at all, and so, yes, Lawrence might have a chance.

Steele also wondered why Lawrence ignored his question about a gunshot being a warning signal? Hadn't the man heard him? But Steele knew he had, and had chosen to ignore the question.

What was going on? Steele thought. Could he expect a shot in the back—or worse?

Chapter Four

The next day there was much talk about Steele and Lawrence's faces.

"I tripped and fell on rocks," explained Steele. He didn't know—or care—what Lawrence's story was.

Ezra White was not fooled.

"You fought over my daughter," he said to Steele when they were alone. "I could see it coming."

"No."

"Yes."

"Well, maybe, partly. Lawrence swung first, though."

"Why, don't you like my daughter?"

"Of course," Steele responded. "Only I never figured on a fight, Mr. White."

"It's Ezra, to my future son-in-law."

Steele felt his face grow hot. "Now, say, I never thought about that. I'm sure Miss White hasn't, either."

"Well, I have, and the father still has a say in these things. There is a tradition, you know." Steele couldn't tell if White was teasing or not.

"Look at it this way," the professor went on. "You could do worse, and I know she could." He nodded toward the head of the train, where a black-clad figure rode, dashing in his saddle.

"Does she like him?" Steele knew she did, but the question popped out.

"Well, he is a looker, enough to turn a young girl's head." White replied. "He's a bit too much for me though. Phony."

"Yeah," Steele's voice trailed off, overcome by jealousy.

As Elizabeth approached, White said hastily, "Our little talk is confidential, Steele. She is not one to let me interfere in her private life."

"I thought you said fathers have a right to choose husbands?" Steele couldn't resist.

"Huh, ah . . . ," but by then Elizabeth had caught up with them.

She was horrified by the sight of Steele's swollen face.

"All I can say is you were mighty clumsy in those rocks." She stared at him. "That doesn't seem like you, Steele. Now," she continued with a glance at Lawrence, down the train, "isn't it odd that you two should both land on your faces?"

"Oh, did he fall, too?" Steele asked.

"I think you know better." Elizabeth paused. "Don't either of you indulge in manly fantasies over me." She said. "I will make my own choice, if the time comes, and the choice doesn't necessarily mean you—in spite of what my father thinks."

"Yes, ma'am," Steele replied.

She smiled, and her voice softened. "Do be careful, Steele."

He rode in the rear of the train that day to keep watch. There had been signs of Indians, but there was no need to alarm the party.

There were times when he saw a suspicious movement in the distance, but it was so far that he was unsure if the movement belonged to Indians or animals. Still, remembering his run-in with Two Dogs, he remained alert.

The sun was just tilting over its apex, and sliding toward its evening couch, when the Indians came. There were ten, and Steele recognized Two Dogs at once. The young war chief sat on his horse as straight as a Ponderosa pine, and his dark eyes were still unreadable. He gave no sign of knowing Steele, nor did Steele strike up a friendly conversation about the good old days up on the Milk. He waited warily.

They had approached from the rear, and Steele cried for the train to halt. Lawrence galloped on his horse over to Two Dogs. He raised his hand, palm outward, in a sign of friendly greeting.

"We come in peace." he said.

Two Dogs did not answer. He stared at him with hard eyes for several moments, then pointed at the cattle.

"We do not have many," Lawrence said.

"Two," was the response.

Others had joined from the wagon. "We ain't got enough cattle to give 'em any," protested a fellow Steele knew as Jacobs.

"I'd advise giving away the cattle," said Lawrence. "It's a tribute to them for traveling through their land. We give them cattle now, or they will steal it at night—with a fight."

There was a quick consultation among the whites. The wagon train had twenty cows, and two could be spared. But a raid, which could result in the loss of more—including lives—was unthinkable. The Indians were a mean-looking lot, Cheyennes all, some with notched feathers in their black hair. Two Dogs wore three of these notched feathers, and Steele happened to know the notches counted for the number of enemies slain. Even a greenhorn could see what the answer had to be.

"Okay, two," muttered Jacobs, "but only two. I don't like being robbed."

"They think they are being robbed," Steele said.

"What do you mean?"

"The Black Hills is their territory, guaranteed

to them by the United States government, but here we are taking it."

"We're just miners. We ain't after homesteads."

"Mining claims are the same to Indians. We're still taking something from their land," Steele said.

"Well, bushwah," grunted Jacobs, "we got clearance from the government, right, Lawrence?"

"Right," agreed the wagon boss, but he didn't sound right to Steele. Too smooth, too quick. And as his band was heading over to cut out the beeves, Steele noticed Two Dogs give Lawrence a quick glance. The Indian's opaque eyes opened briefly in a flash of recognition. They knew each other, Steele realized. There was no harm in that; many whites and Indians knew each other. But that Lawrence didn't want the others to know he was acquainted with the Indian bothered Steele. Something wasn't right. He couldn't prove anything, but Steele felt negatives in his bones.

As Two Dogs was leaving, his dark eyes focused briefly on Steele. Steele was surprised to see a sparkle of recognition, and then more surprised to catch an almost imperceptible nod of respect. Then Two Dogs turned away, and led his band off with the beeves.

Apparently Two Dogs had been impressed by the lone white man at Milk River. Steele remembered the war chief's derisive laughter as he teased his braves.

That was good, but not good enough to dissolve Steele's feeling that trouble lay ahead. A raid, perhaps? And if so, when? Steele considered asking Lawrence if he thought there would be more trouble, but changed his mind. After what he'd seen pass between Two Dogs and the wagon boss, Steele distrusted Lawrence more than ever.

Two days after the Indian visit, the party arrived at Candy Mountain.

There were grumbles.

"Looks like any other hill to me," protested a sturdy chap named Crisp. "Lots of trees, a few streams."

"Those streams are what you want," Lawrence assured him. "That's where the gold is."

"Yeah, well, looks pretty ordinary."

"And you have lots of trees for cabins," Lawrence went on.

"Cabins?" Elizabeth was struck by the remark. "Why cabins?"

"It's late October, and winter will be behind the next hard storm. If you are to prospect this area thoroughly—and I assume you will—you'll have to stay the winter."

"You never said nothing about winter," Jacobs yelled.

"I assumed you knew," was Lawrence's quick reply.

"You assumed too much," Crisp said.

"No," Lawrence told him evenly, "I did not. You must have known winter comes to this country pretty early. If you didn't, I apologize. I should have said something."

"Yes," Ezra White put in, "you should have, but you didn't. The way I see it, it's not a big matter. We *are* going to stay, right?" A crowd had gathered, and he looked at them in a kind of dare. "I'm for it."

"Can't see any way out," grumbled Crisp.

And that was the general opinion.

But Steele didn't want to let the trail guide off so easily. "I haven't seen signs of other parties," he told Lawrence. "If Candy Mountain is so good, there should be at least some sign."

"This is a big lump of a hill, friend," Lawrence replied. "Might be days to the nearest digs."

"Even at that, I think we should find them. Maybe we can learn something worthwhile."

"No use doing that. If anybody found gold, do you think they'd tell? By no means! They'd keep it secret. Take my word, folks, there's gold here."

That ended the discussion. The would-be miners unloaded their wagons, and pitched their tents. Because of the Indian situation, guards were posted day and night, while groups went out to prospect the land. Ledges were examined for veins of gold-bearing quartz. Streams were panned, and some gold dust was found. There was just enough "color," as the stream gold was called, to encourage the prospectors.

"Just might be worthwhile" admitted Jacobs and Crisp, somewhat cheered after a gloomy time thinking of spending the winter in the area.

Lawrence strolled around, seeming very pleased with himself, saying, "See? You'll all make it big, I'm sure."

Steele wondered about the man. He was either one of the best wagon bosses in the West, or the best liar. In the evenings, much to Steele's exasperation, the man showed off his expertise with a harmonica. He led the way at camp sing-alongs, and Steele saw that Elizabeth was impressed. He, himself, couldn't play two nails together, but Lawrence was good. Lawrence also owned a fine baritone voice, and when somebody else played an instrument, he sang solos for the crowd. Steele was not, in the final analysis, a social man. Lawrence was, and his stock with the group was high.

"He's good, all right," admitted White. "The man got us here, dealt with the Indians, looks like we might even find some gold. He's good, all right, so why is it I don't like him?"

Steele was gratified. "You mean I'm not alone?"

"He's too smooth for me. I've met a lot of them in my profession, and Pat Lawrence can stand with the best. All surface, not much underneath."

"Elizabeth—" Steele started, to say, then stopped abruptly.

"She has a mind of her own. She's struck by his charm, certainly, but don't worry. She really feels the same as I do about him."

"Don't seem like it," muttered Steele.

"What's that?"

"I'd say we better get started on those cabins. We've been here two weeks, and not a log cut yet."

Ezra White grinned. "That's what I thought you said."

On the morning of the third week, after the camp had been set, Lawrence announced he was leaving for Deadwood.

"Have to get more supplies," he informed the startled prospectors. "And report to Red Clark about our progress."

There were protests.

"What about Indians?" Jacobs said. "We don't know how to deal with them. You do."

"Oh, they won't return," Lawrence breezily replied. "They'd have done it by now."

"We've got enough supplies, to last six months," said Crisp.

"You might be here longer," Lawrence responded. "No. I'm leaving for more groceries. After all, you are my responsibility."

"And I'd better let the military know where we are, too," he added.

"If they know we are here, they'll make us leave," said White.

"No. Not right now. The military doesn't know what way to jump. The government is negotiating with the Indians. In the meantime, matters are at a standstill."

With that, Lawrence mounted his horse and headed down the back trail, when Jacobs shouted, "Hey, we ain't got a map. If you don't get back, how do we know which way is out?"

Lawrence rode on, and the question died in the still air.

"He heard," said White.

"Yes, he did," agreed Steele. Then he snapped into action and called for a meeting that night.

"We better start building our cabins now," he said when everyone gathered. "Cold weather is not around the corner; it is here. We don't want to get caught in a blizzard."

"Who are you to tell us what to do?" said a voice.

"Nobody. But I've had experience in this country, and I'm just giving advice. Build now or freeze later."

The wagoneers knew he was right. Ice was forming on the streams, and once they were frozen, prospecting for gold, in the stream beds would be finished.

Steele really wanted to build a fort. He wanted a settlement with a strong log barricade protecting it from a possible raid, but he didn't want to alarm the easterners. He decided to mention the barricade idea after the cabins were built. The cabins themselves would have to serve as forts in case of emergency.

He was too late. The Indian raid came early the second morning after Lawrence departed. Steele was standing watch near the south end of the wagons, when he saw Cheyenne slipping through the grass. He hollered, "Indians!" and fired his pistol.

The men in the party grabbed their firearms and took appointed posts. The wagons had been arranged in a half circle, not the full circle of the open plains, because, Lawrence said, there wasn't room. It was not a good defensive position, because the wagons were vulnerable to attack on the entire southwest side.

"Lawrence has done his work well," Steele growled as White took a stance by his side.

"Very well," agreed White. "He's a regular Benedict Arnold."

"Who?"

"Read history and find out," was White's unhelpful reply.

By then guns on both sides were blaring. White carried a .45–70 single-shot carbine. He aimed and fired, and then loaded and fired again. His was smiling, and he winked at Steele. "This," he said softly, "is what I call living to the full—I'm testing my whole being, boy, and find I'm not afraid. It's good to know." Then he fired again.

Elizabeth had no weapon, but she clutched a butcher knife, and stood by her father. *No man, will ever hurt them and live to walk away,* thought Steele

He turned his attention to the defenses of the group, and raced along, bent low, checking for problems. As far as the people were concerned, there were no problems. They were firing coolly, and standing ground. But they were badly exposed to the southwest, and Steele realized it wouldn't be long before they were cut down.

As he checked, he also fired at the enemy, now not so far away that his pistol couldn't reach them. He saw Two Dogs, which was no surprise, but he also saw two light-colored bodies—too light, he thought, to be Indians.

"Must be a hundred," yelled Jacobs.

"Two hundred," cried Crisp, upping the ante.

There were twenty men and eleven women in the white party. None of them, except himself, Steele noted, experienced, but every one of them was fighting back. Aim, fire, aim, fire. Steele was surprised to realize he felt pride being in their company. *They were green as spring corn, but tough as buffalo hide,* he thought. These people were not apt to be driven off easily, but something had to be done to close off the open southwest side.

"Hitch the horses to wagons one, two, three, and four," he yelled.

"*Now?*" came the astounded response. "Man, we'll be killed fooling around with them horses."

"You'll be killed if you don't get some protection on that open side," Steele said grimly. "Now get going. Quick!"

"Looky here," protested one of the younger men, "we don't take orders . . ."

A shot from Steele's .44, ripped a hole in the wagon boards next to the youth's head. The young man squawked, and dove for harnesses and horses.

"Five or six of you help," ordered Steele. "Quick."

He shoved his pistol back in its holster, and grabbed a harness himself. Several men pitched in.

"The rest of you fire at anything you see out there—especially if you see light skin."

The sun shots increased, and smoke hung heavily in the air. The horses were harnessed, but not without loss. Two men were injured and two horses were killed. After the horses were hitched, the wagons were quickly drawn into place. A makeshift fort was formed. They were still vulnerable, but Steele was satisfied with their added protection.

He positioned himself with Elizabeth and Ezra, aiming his .44 at anything moving beyond the wagons.

The shooting swelled and ebbed like a tide, and the hills shook with vibrating echos. Whites were hit, Indians fell, but Steele noted the enemy didn't try to charge. The Indians were leery of this stubborn resistance, and were fighting from a distance.

"I want to get closer," Steele said to Elizabeth.

"You'll be killed," she objected, and Steele was pleased to see concern in her eyes.

Jacobs was shooting in the next wagon.

"You take over," Steele shouted, "if I don't get back."

"Where are you going?" Jacobs replied, surprised.

Steele didn't answer, but under cover of an especially violent outburst of shots from both sides, he dashed into the forest. Blue powder smoke partially obscured his move, but he flopped behind a giant pine, and lay very still.

He knew he was being foolish. If the Indians saw him, he'd be dead in seconds. Worse, they might take him alive, and have their fun later— a thought that chilled Steele. Still, he had to prove his suspicions.

The closest Indian was fifty feet away. Steele watched as the Indian loaded his single-shot rifle, but Steele didn't dare give his position away by attacking the warrior. His mission wasn't to kill the enemy, but to learn who the two white-skinned Indians were.

He crept forward, passing behind the Indian. Before Steele had gone a hundred feet, he saw who he was looking for. Lawrence had apparently shaved his mustache. He was stripped to the waist and wore buckskin trousers. His hair was dark like the Indians and, except for skin color, he looked just like an Indian.

Steele angered, and acted foolishly again. "Lawrence!" he shouted.

The "Indian" whirled, firing at the same time. Steele felt the bullet graze his arm, then he closed with Lawrence. There was no room for firearms, and they were dropped, knives drawn. They knew the other was an even match, but this was a battle to the death.

Suddenly Steele realized the firing had stopped. Steele glanced around. Two Dogs watched them with a cocked Springfield. Steele knew then even if he killed Lawrence, he was a dead man himself. Before he could react he saw Red Clark. Steele's suspicions were confirmed; he and his companions on the wagon train had been tricked. This raid was the payoff.

There was no time for thought. Lawrence, his white, even teeth lighting up a triumphant grin, lunged. He held a Bowie knife, huge compared to Steele's six-inch skinning knife, used for dressing animals killed for food.

He dodged Lawrence's thrust, backed off, circled, and lunged himself. His knife was easily parried by the Bowie, and the two men closed again. Lawrence jabbed several times, but Steele managed to avoid the blade. The anger of each man was such that care was finally thrown to the winds. Each parried and slashed and jabbed, reaching for the heart, but they were as skilled with knives as they were with fists.

"If you don't get him, Lawrence, I will!"

shouted Clark. He cocked his own weapon, and aimed at Steele.

On top of Clark's threat came Two Dogs' voice. "You shoot him, and I'll kill you."

"But he's our enemy!"

"When two men fight, it is their fight not ours. Afterwards," the war chief shrugged, "then we see." He hefted his own rifle.

"I say we kill him now!" growled Clark.

Two Dogs turned on him. "You say this would be an easy fight, like the others. It is not. White men fight good. Many braves hurt."

"We got 'em on the run," Clark argued. "Just a little more time, and the wagons are ours." He was sly. "And many weapons for you."

Two Dogs didn't answer. He turned his attention back to the two battling men, and Clark wasn't sure where he stood with the Indian chief. But he did lower his weapon.

Steele realized that unless he escaped, he would be killed by either Two Dogs or Clark. Even if he defeated Lawrence, there was only one end for himself. He decided to take desperate measures.

He lunged at Lawrence, as he had a dozen

times. His foe leapt aside, but Steele plunged on. Instead of turning to fight, he kept going. He plowed through trees, and ran for the wagons. Shouts and shots followed him, and he heard bullets whine overhead, thunking into the trees. Some of the Indians were laughing. They appreciated that sort of trick, that kind of bravado. Even so, Steele knew he was a dead man if he was caught.

He ran like a deer. When he burst into the clearing, at the rim of the forest, the wagoneers saw him. They immediately set up a burst of covering fire that kept the Cheyenne back. The fleeing man literally dove behind Ezra White's wagon. He was up åt once, snatched a rifle, and joined the battle.

Then, suddenly, it was over. There was no return firing from the woods. Silence dropped like a soothing, soft blanket over the region. The Indians were either gone or planning another strategy.

In the silence of the moment Steele had time to look around. His eyes sought Elizabeth and found, instead, the still body of her father. His daughter crouched next to him.

"He's dead," she said bitterly.

Steele approached the older man. He'd been shot through the temple, and death had come instantly.

Sadness and anger prompted Steele to blurt, "Well, my girl, you can thank your fancy frontiersman for this. Might have been one of his bullets that killed your father."

The girl turned on him, her voice accusing. "It's your fault," she said. "If you hadn't fired that first shot, we might have not had a fight at all. You are responsible for my father's death."

Chapter Five

Steele's was shocked. "Girl, you're crazy!" he shouted.

"If you hadn't shot at them," "they might not have fired back." The girl was so angry and grief-stricken, she could hardly speak.

"No." Steele's voice softened. He was slightly ashamed of his outburst. "Those Indians were after our scalps, and all we own here."

Elizabeth White glared, her face pale and her lips tight. "I hate you, Steele. Get out of here," she hissed.

Steele left, seeing that there was no reasoning with her. Oddly, he wanted to take her in his arms and comfort her, but she hated him.

As he left, he said to the crowd that had gathered, "I have reason to believe there were not only Indians in that bunch."

"What do you mean?" asked Jacobs. "They all looked alike to me."

"The reason I sneaked over to their side like I did wasn't to play war, but to make sure of what I suspected. Our stalwart leader, Pat Lawrence, and our supplier, Red Clark, were with the Cheyenne."

"Nonsense!" shouted Crisp, "I didn't see anybody who looked like either of them."

"They were stripped down to look like Indians. They are what's known in this country as renegades."

"Renegades?" asked Jacobs.

"Whites who join Indian raiding parties to share in the spoils. They often know where the spoils are, and lead the Indians to them."

"I didn't see nobody with a mustache like Pat's," said a younger man, named Tom.

"Could have shaved it off."

Tom shook his head. "Not likely. He was proud of that lip warmer, I can tell you."

"But if that's the case," added another young man named Pete, "then they both ought to be brought to justice."

Steele liked both men. They had been brave in the fight, both blazing away, Pete even smiling, as if he enjoyed a good battle.

"In time, they will," Steele said.

"How do you know?"

"Because, I'll see to it."

"But, you said 'in time.' What kind of time?"

"Don't know for sure." Steele glanced at the yellowing trees. "It is late in the year. If we are to stay, and we've agreed we would, we better build a fort." He was not reluctant to use the word now. "Maybe, after that, I'll have a look for them."

"I don't think we should wait," said Tom.

"Meaning?" asked Steele.

"They are still nearby, I'll wager. I think we better get them now."

"I'd advise against it."

"Why, you scared?"

Steele gave way to irritation. "No," he snapped, "but they are waiting, undecided whether to attack again. If they catch you— well, it won't be a Sunday school picnic."

"Huh, we beat 'em once, they wasn't so much." He looked at Pete. "How's about it?"

Elizabeth spoke up. "Let them go," she said with venom. "Maybe they'll kill a few, and get revenge for my father." Her manner remained cold, and she refused to look at Steele.

The two mounted their horses, and, waving their hats in bravado, set off. Steele watched with dread. There was nothing he could do to stop them, and he felt dark premonitions.

The group returned to their wounded. Ezra White had been the only death, though there were some painful wounds. Fortunately, fire arrows had not been used, probably, Steele guessed, on the direction of the white leaders who didn't want their merchandise ruined. But water casks had been smashed, wagon wheels broken, two horses and two cows dead. Still, they'd were lucky. There could have been a slaughter of the entire wagon train. Steele knew neither Clark nor Lawrence wanted witnesses.

Steele walked through camp assessing the damage. He admired the people, for they had battled well. They had not panicked in the face of some of the most deadly warriors on the Plains.

Steele had always been a loner. He wasn't against people but he never felt like he belonged with anyone. These people came from a different life than Steele, but nothing had changed. They had been tested and survived well. Steele knew he was among his own kind now—a loner no more.

"Do you think they'll come back?" one of the women asked.

"I don't know," he replied honestly. "But we'll have to be ready."

"I am," said the woman, and she patted her rifle.

He set guards out, and brought the cattle and horses inside the enclosure. The logs were used to close the spaces between the wagons.

"That ought to hold the rascals," Crisp said, satisfied.

"Don't be too sure," Steele said. "Those rascals, as you call them, can creep up on us silent as a rattler."

He was worried about the two young men, Pete and Tom. If they were lucky, the Indians did leave. He had no idea how many Cheyenne braves were lost, but if the list was long, the

Indians would move on. If there was a big war coming, as Two Dogs claimed, the Cheyenne would need all their braves to fight. They would not allow heavy losses of life in small battles like this. Perhaps there was hope for the two brash whites.

He was wrong. That evening, the group was startled by screams in the distance.

"What, what was that?" Jacobs cried.

"I don't know," Steele lied. He knew exactly what was happening. The Indians were torturing white captives.

The screams continued, and the camp listened quietly. The last rays of the sun turned the western sky blood red, and the hills stood silhouetted against the sky like tombstones. Men figured their rifles nervously.

"It's them, isn't it?" Crisp asked, finally. "The boys?"

"Yes," Steele said. "It's them."

He went to Elizabeth's wagon, concerned. Her father's body was lying under a blanket, and she was sitting near him, her face turned toward the piercing screams.

"My God," she whispered. "What's going

on?" There was no hate in her eyes, only horror. "Do those—could that be Pete and Tom?"

Steele nodded. "The Indians have them."

"But why torture them?"

"It's the Indian way. They are sending us a warning, and having fun."

"*Fun!*"

The girl shivered silently. The screams continued, at times lapsing into maniacal laughter. Then the cries seemed to gurgle and choke off as if flooded with liquid.

Jacobs came to the wagon, clutching his weapon. "By heaven, I'm going to help those boys," he declared.

Others appeared, their faces grim.

"We've got to do something," Crisp said.

Steele drew his pistol, cocked it, but held the muzzle down.

"The first man who leaves will be shot," he said quietly.

The men stared at him in disbelief. "You can't mean it," one said. "It's our duty to help them."

For an answer, Steele shot into the air. The sound echoed.

The group was stunned.

Pale-faced, Jacobs said, "You would do it," he whispered. "You would kill me?"

Steele, hard-eyed, studied the man. He liked both Jacobs and Crisp. Both had shown ability and common sense. As green as they were, they took to the country easily.

"No," said Steele, "I would not kill you. But I am ordering you not to go out there. There is nothing you can do, and you will get the same."

Crisp bristled. "What do you mean, you're 'ordering' us not to go out there? You aren't leader here."

"Yes," Steele informed him, "I am. Listen, I know Indians, I know western ways. None of you do. I'm going to use what I know, and maybe save our skins. If you don't like it, you're welcome to move on. But I am now the wagon boss; if you stay you will listen to me."

Silence greeted this announcement. The cries of the two captives were weakening, faint flutters in the darkening sky.

Steele wondered what would happen next. There were good men in the outfit, men who could easily sway the situation away from him. It was a moment of decision, but he faced the group, with determination. He slid the pistol back in its holster, and waited.

After several minutes of silence, Steele said, "We will post guards tonight, very heavy guards."

This was the test.

Jacobs said, "I'll take the first watch. Who will stand with me?"

Several more volunteered for different times of the night, and Steele took the last watch. He was relieved that matters turned out as they did. He had made a bold play, but he knew he was the man for the job.

Elizabeth watched the proceedings silently. She found herself admiring Steele's style. There was no doubt in her mind, after hearing the agony of Pete and Tom, that the Indians would have attacked with or without Steele's warning shot. Had the Indians won, she was certain now, there would have been a massacre.

It was difficult for her to accept that the courtly Pat Lawrence had been among them.

Yet, Steele had risked his life to find out. A man who would do that would know what he'd seen. If he said he saw Lawrence and Clark, he probably did. Yet, none of the Indians she'd seen had a mustache. From what she'd heard, they did not grow heavy facial hair, and Lawrence sprouted that luxurious beauty. But it was possible, she knew, that he could have shaved it off so as not to be recognized.

Elizabeth looked at the blanket-covered figure of her father sadly. If he'd remained in Boston, he'd still be very much alive. He used to say Indian raids didn't exist. Massacres, he said, as many did, were the figment of writers' imaginations. There were no such things as massacres and scalpings and torture, he believed.

Her father had been wrong. The West, while not as wild as writers would have easterners believe, was wild enough. It had killed her father. Would he have come West had he believed all he read? she wondered. Yes she knew he would have made the trip. Her father wanted a different life. He needed to get away from cobblestoned streets, multi-storied buildings, prejudiced academics. He was stifled by civilization—safe, but stifled. He wanted to touch the earth, to feel life with his fingers, not his mind alone. He had recently told her that he was a different man, that he felt whole and real. No, Elizabeth concluded, he would not have changed things at all. The fact that he'd been killed was a tragic end to a good life, and yet Elizabeth knew, if her father could speak to her, he would say, "I have lived more than most, for I was a whole man, no matter how briefly. Death, my dear, is part of life."

Elizabeth's thoughts drifted to her own life. She was single, city bred, and now, without her father, alone. Should she stay in the West now that her father was dead, or return to the East? She could teach. Her father had a pension that she would inherit. She could live comfortably.

The idea was tempting—but did she really want a life like that? It was safe, but was she interested in safety? If Lawrence and Clark were responsible for her father's death, and if they were among the Indians and helped plan the raid, she wanted to know. If they were, indeed, among the Indians, she wanted to deal with them personally—as personal as a bullet or a hangman's noose could make it.

She stood up, and threw more wood on the fire. Return to the East? She had some things to take care of first.

Chapter Six

Across the pine-studded hills, not far from the wagons, the Cheyenne finished their grisly work. Lawrence and Clark, still in their Indian garb, were having a conference.

"Thank heaven that's over," muttered Clark. "I never get used to that screaming."

"You got a soft stomach?" Lawrence grinned, showing his white teeth.

"You cold-blooded fish," grunted his companion. "Do you ever feel any pity at all?"

Lawrence shrugged. "It's a matter of business," he stated.

"Why do they do that?" Clark nodded at the mutilated bodies of Tom and Pete.

"Without arms, legs, or heads, the spirits of the dead can't follow them."

"Gore," muttered Clark. Then he suddenly barked, "Business? This is *business*? What do you mean?"

"That makes two less we will have to fight later."

Clark thought that over, and nodded. "Yeah. When are we going to hit again?"

"Not now. They're waiting for us. Steele will keep them on their toes." Lawrence's lips, thin without the mustache, tightened. "He has got to go."

"Do you think he recognized us?"

"Oh, yes, but he won't convince the others. They like me. I'm their hero frontiersman."

Lawrence's voice had dropped to a heavy contempt. He glared in the direction of the wagon train. "Greenhorn fools."

"So," said Clark, "what's next?"

"We'll go back to Deadwood. You can work up more parties, and I'll bring supplies back to Candy Mountain. Got to do that now, in order to keep control." He glared toward the white contingent again. "None of this would be necessary if not for that vagabond Steele. Unlucky day when we took him in. I'll get him first." Lawrence's face darkened. "I'll get Steele."

Lawrence went to his saddlebags, and pulled out his dashing mustache. He shaped it under his nose carefully, patting it down firmly.

"If that ain't something to see," remarked Clark. "A naked Indian with a handlebar mustache."

"This little bit of hair has served us well." Lawrence laughed. "Makes me look quite the fellow, eh?"

The two dressed in their civilian clothes, and went to the Cheyenne Village to see Two Dogs. The young chief was resting in front of his fire with several braves. Lawrence realized that they'd been having a conference of their own.

"Many warrior hurt in fight, and two die," the chief said, without a sign of friendly greeting.

"They were good men, and I am sorry," replied Lawrence.

"You are not sorry for my people, only that you did not get your wagons and supplies back."

"Chief, I am a businessman. You would have received your share, but it went wrong. I have always been honest with you."

Two Dogs nodded, his eyes dark "What now, white man?"

"We must wait. We will strike when snow falls," said Lawrence.

"And that white man who came to our fighting place, he will know you."

"I will take care of him."

Two Dogs shook his head. "He is a man of courage. Good man. Worthy enemy."

Lawrence flushed. He knew he was being told that he was not as good a man as Steele.

"I'll handle him," he vowed stiffly. "Don't worry about him."

"I don't worry. *You* worry. You worry about him and you worry about me. I have many wounded," he repeated. "Two dead. You said none would die."

There was a threatening tone in Two Dogs' voice that neither of the white men liked. Their connection with the chief was vital to their bloody schemes.

"We'll get him," Lawrence quickly assured

the chief. "We will get those in the wagon train, too, and they will pay for your dead."

"That is good."

Lawrence and Clark, sensed that it was time to leave. Two Dogs gazed after them as they trotted out of the village. He did not like them either, and thought they were traitors to their own kind. But he needed them. He needed weapons. War, he thought, was terribly strange; it brought good and bad men together on the same side.

He rose, but his mind was still full. *Gold*! The yellow rocks and dust stuck in the creeks and ledges of the Black Hills was causing all the trouble. The white man's government had said no whites would be allowed into the Hills, but gold brought them by the hundreds. The U.S. Army could not keep them out, so it was up to the Indians. The Black Hills were one of the last good hunting grounds, and must be saved. All of the Indians—Sioux, Cheyenne, Crow—all the tribes were talking. They agreed the white man must be stopped. In the spring there would be a big meeting at the Little Big Horn River, and a plan would be made. . . .

* * *

Lawrence and Clark trotted along, discussing the meeting.

"I don't like the way Two Dogs looked at us," said Clark.

"Don't worry about him." Lawrence spat into the alkali ground. "He needs us. He'll come around."

Lawrence had already formed his plan. He would boldly return to Candy Mountain. Aside from the wagons, there were two things he wanted—Steele's life, and Elizabeth. She had looked on him with favor before he left. He would see to it that she was spared when the next battle erupted. Perhaps he should even woo her now, and take her back to Deadwood, before killing the other members of the wagon train. Lawrence nodded to himself. That would be best.

Clark's aims were more straightforward. All he wanted were his goods back. He had sold the same merchandise three times, making enormous profits each time Two Dogs wiped out an expedition. He smiled happily. He was sure everything would work out well. You had to expect setbacks now and then. They'd get that Candy Mountain bunch when the snow was on the ground. They'd get them good. Especially that Texas tramp, Steele.

The man both Lawrence and Carter hated was not wasting time preparing the wagon train for winter. Having taken charge, he had started building a fortified village. Before it was completed, Pat Lawrence returned with several wagons of additional supplies. He was furious.

"Who authorized a fort?" he demanded. "Cabins are enough."

"I did," Steele told him.

"You? You're nothing in this outfit!"

"No," Steele corrected. "You are wrong. I've taken your place."

Jacobs and Crisp appeared with a number of others.

"We needed a leader and Steele knows what he's doing," Crisp said. "Where were you when the Indians attacked us?" he asked.

The crowd was silent, waiting for an answer.

Lawrence acted surprised. "Attack?" His eyes traveled the length of the wagons. "All seems to be well. Was anybody hurt?"

"My father was killed," said Elizabeth. "You said there'd be no danger from Indians."

"I had no idea," Lawrence said gently. "I'm so sorry about your father, Elizabeth. What a terrible thing."

"I think that you were with the Indians," Steele said.

"What do you mean? How dare you make such an accusation!" Lawrence shouted.

"I fought you, Lawrence."

"Impossible."

"You were with them."

"Are you calling me a liar?"

"Yes, and a murderer as well."

Lawrence realized that the showdown was at hand.

"Make up your minds," he declared to the gathering crowd. "Can't be two of us running the show."

"You wasn't going to stay, anyhow," said Crisp.

"That's right. You was just going to bring supplies, then skeedaddle," Jacobs said.

"You need me," Lawrence said.

"No," said Crisp. "We don't."

"Meaning?"

"That means you can go or stay, but if you stay, you are no longer leader of this party."

"This is your doing," Lawrence growled Steele.

"No, it's yours. You fought on the Indian side."

Lawrence dropped his hand close to his ivory-handled pistol. "I ought to . . ."

"You ought to what, renegade."

"*Renegade*! You can't prove that!"

"Oh, yes I can, and you know how."

Lawrence was swift. His action was smooth, nothing wasted, but Steele was swifter. His weapon was out of its holster, and cocked, before Lawrence's cleared leather. The man with the handsome mustache stared death in the eye.

But Steele didn't pull the trigger. He had a better plan. If punishment were to be given, it would be best the whole group decided how to give it. Now it was time to prove Lawrence's guilt. He walked over to the man. "Drop your weapon," Steele said.

Lawrence hesitated, hate in his eyes.

"Now!" Steele centered the barrel of his Colt on the other man's chest.

The pistol hit the ground. Then Steele reached up and ripped the false mustache from Lawrence's lip.

The crowd gasped.

"Well, for pity's sakes." Jacobs stared at the hairpiece, fascinated.

Elizabeth, realizing the finality of Steele's action, said mockingly, "Well, so much for the frontiersman."

"So, you *were* with the Indians," whispered Crisp.

The crowd stiffened collectively. Then somebody said, "Get a rope."

But Lawrence was not about to be hanged. He jumped onto his horse and fled. He disappeared into the trees.

"We'll follow," said Jacobs.

"Don't," advised Steele.

"But he's a traitor, a killer. He wanted to wipe us out!" protested Crisp. "He deserves to be hanged."

"Remember what we saw when we went to find Pete and Tom?"

Crisp simmered down.

"There could be another war party out there waiting." Steele turned to the others. "Get your weapons, and be ready," he instructed. "If nothing happens, fine. If it does, rip into them."

"Hey," cried one of the men on the newly arrived supply train, "what about us? We was just hired to drive the wagons."

"Turn them around," said Steele, "and go back where you got them."

"I'd vote no on that," said Jacobs.

"Meaning?"

"As long as the stuff is here, let's keep it. We'll pay later." He grinned. "Maybe. The new supplies will make up for the awful things that man has done."

"And, don't forget Clark," Steele reminded him.

"Not ever."

"Suit yourself," said Steele. "You teamsters are welcome here overnight. Tomorrow, you git."

"Good enough," growled the speaker. "I got no wish t' stay."

* * *

The fort was completed just before the heavy snow fell. The group named it Fort White, in honor of Elizabeth's father.

"He gave his life fighting for all of us," said Crisp. "It's the least we can do in his memory."

Elizabeth decided to move in with Jacobs and his family. His wife, a pleasant woman named Emily, and two sons, both about Pete and Tom's age, were an easy family to adjust to, and made her feel at home. But she had one problem.

"My father and I came here to prospect, and I want to carry on," she told Steele one day. "But I don't know the first thing about gold."

"You can come with me," said Steele. "I know a little about panning the streams."

"Or you can come with me," Jacobs added with a rueful grin, "but I know nothing."

Elizabeth ended up going with both men. The entire group split up into small cadres of two or three, heading out in different areas to search for the stuff that made kings rich—but there was a difference. What one found would be shared by all.

"We are in this together," Jacobs stated at a meeting, "and we either go broke or make something together."

The party searched for gold until the streams froze over.

"We'll just hold on until spring," Steele said. "Maybe we can do some hard-rock prospecting, quartz in the ledges, on warm days. Freezing doesn't hurt quartz," he said with a grin. He paused. "We'll keep guards posted constantly. We simply can't trust Lawrence not to come back with Two Dogs."

There were angry growls of assent at this, but Leary, who hadn't participated before, except as a rifleman, objected.

"Them redskins won't attack in winter," he insisted.

"Do you know they won't?" asked Steele.

"Nobody but a fool would come through them blizzards and snow."

"And Indians—they aren't fools. The guard duty stands."

When the attack came on an unexpected moment, a Sunday, it arrived in the most horrible way.

Leary had been sent out to hunt elk, since the meat supply was low. He was returned midday. He was tied face down in the saddle, hands and feet strapped under his mount's stomach to keep him from sliding off. There were three arrows in his back, and he'd been scalped. His horse followed his scent back home, bringing this grisly package with him.

By the time Steele arrived, Leary was placed on the ground. He was frozen stiff, in a curled position.

Steele examined the arrows closely.

"This is the same kind that were used last fall," he decided. "Could be the same tribe back again."

At that moment a fire arrow soared over the barricades. It landed harmlessly, missing any structure.

"This is it!" Steele cried. "Get up there, men, and make sure of your aim!"

Chapter Seven

Steele had drilled the men on what to do in case of an attack. They climbed to platforms high on the barricades, and fired at the shadowy forms closing in.

What Steele couldn't understand was Leary's murder. It clearly gave away the Indians' intent.

"Shows their contempt for us," Jacobs guessed. "They probably got more men, and more firepower."

The air was heavy with blue powder smoke, but Steele saw from his platform the enemy slipping through the trees, drawing ever closer. They were nearly invisible, weaving through the trees like the wind, their position revealed mainly by a moving branch or a cloud of gunpowder smoke.

Elizabeth stood with Steele, firing a Winchester.

"You'll get hurt!" Steele yelled "Or worse. Get down off here."

"I couldn't care less," Elizabeth replied. "I'm after those rascals who killed my father. Lawrence and Clark, particularly, if they are here."

Steele was also trying to locate the con men, but the Indians were dressed in winter clothing, buckskin and furs—no white skins to give the two away.

"I'm with you," he said, and didn't try getting her to safety again. She would do what she wanted, and Steele didn't blame her.

He left his post to check others. Several men had been wounded, and were being cared for by women. The women, however, were not solely nursemaids. They stood at the ramparts with their men, reloading rifles, and taking shots of their own.

The firing increased and Steele began to worry about ammunition.

"Be sure of your targets," he began shouting. "Shoot at flesh and bone only."

The battle was at a standoff. The Indians were not charging. The shots from the white man's tent were too deadly. The would-be miners might have been from the East, but that didn't mean they couldn't shoot.

They were all a cool lot, Steele noted, and he was again proud of them.

When the fire arrows began in earnest, though, he realized the tide could change for the worse. The arrows found marks in roofs, and blazes started.

"Fire brigades!" he shouted. Steele, Elizabeth and several others stepped from the barricades into motion.

A well had been dug in the center of the compound, and a bucket brigade was formed. The hungry flames, like some arrogant dragon, sneered at the water, and chomped at the roofs. The only thing that really satisfied the monster's appetite was the fact the logs were green. Green wood did not succumb so quickly.

Into this dual fight—one with the fires, the other with the Indians—came a familiar voice.

"What do you think of it now, Steele?"

A fur-clad figure stepped into view from behind a large pine. It was Lawrence, false mustache and all. Beside him was Clark.

"You're still the biggest laugh on the Great Plains," Steele shouted.

"You give up, and we'll spare the people," Lawrence said.

"If we give up, you'll leave no witnesses," responded Steele, and he fired at them.

Lawrence and Clark ducked, but Lawrence shouted, "All right—that's the way you want it, that's how you'll get it. Not one will leave alive."

"That—that hateful person!" Elizabeth cried.

In spite of the situation, Steele couldn't help but grin.

"I wish, that you'd watch your language," he said.

"You know perfectly well what I mean," Elizabeth said. "I want that man dead. If he didn't shoot my father personally, he caused the bullet that killed him." She began to cry. "I want him dead, Steele!"

The firing resumed, and Steele saw Two Dogs

directing his warriors. Tactics were being discussed, and it was likely a charge was in mind. Two Dogs wanted the white weapons and ammunition. He might decide to make sacrifices for them. Steele was sure no prisoners would be taken, unless to torture them.

Smoke from the fires was spreading, engulfing the entire battleground, and visibility was almost nil. Steele was certain the Indians would charge under its cover, "Keep your eyes peeled, and your weapons cocked!" he shouted. "Look for a charge."

As if in response, a dark face appeared at the top of the wall. It was shot off at once, but more faces appeared; then entire figures dropped into the compound.

A buck-skinned figure flung himself on Steele. It was Two Dogs. Steele swung the rifle he'd been using, and pulled the trigger. It clicked on an empty chamber. Two Dogs shook his head, threw his rifle down, and pulled a knife from his belt.

"For you and me." He said, "Man to man, this is the way it should be."

Steele drew his own knife, aware of the chaos

around him. He glanced for Elizabeth, but couldn't see ten feet because of the smoke. Two Dogs lunged at him. Steele parried, and thrust back. Two Dogs circled around Steele. He respected the ability of a man who could infiltrate battle lines as Steele had done during the last fight. Here was a worthwhile white adversary.

Suddenly, above the shouts and cries of battle, an Indian voice gave words to a short sentence. The words were filled with frustration and anger, but immediately after that, the Indians disappeared. Two Dogs, his face twisted in disappointment, cried, "We will meet again, Steele!"

Steele, utterly baffled by this change in events, nodded. "Yes, because I will search for the two white traitors, and kill them. You know who I mean, Two Dogs."

Two Dogs vanished into the smoke, and Steele did not attempt to follow. Instead, he searched for Elizabeth. He found her, as the smoke cleared briefly under a gust of wind, at their station by the barricade. She knew nothing of his fight with Two Dogs.

"Where have you been?" she cried excitedly. "I think we have them on the run."

"Yes," replied Steele, and an incongruous thought entered his mind. At that moment, he'd never seen a more beautiful woman than Elizabeth White. "We beat them" he went on, "but I don't know why."

"Because of the way we fought back," Elizabeth said proudly.

"Yes . . . but I think there is more to it."

Half a dozen men were placed on guard around the inner circumference of the fort, and the rest fought the fires. They were brought under control with concentrated effort, thanks to the green building materials, and plenty of water. Smoke damage was the worst kind.

The fire had no sooner been conquered than the answer to the disappearance of the Indians appeared. A troop of U.S. Cavalry rode in. At its head was a captain, who was mighty irritable.

"What is this place?" the angry captain asked the milling miners.

"Fort White," answered Jacobs. "And thank God you came in time!"

The captain's face was bright red in wrath. "We heard the battle, all right. I'm looking for an Indian named Two Dogs."

"Well, you're close," Steele said.

"You saw him?"

"Him and fifty other braves, plus a couple of white renegades."

"Lawrence and Clark?"

"The same."

The captain swore. "Now you scared 'em off, and I suppose I'll never get 'em!"

"Sorry about that, but we had to save our lives, Captain."

The man in the blue uniform relaxed a bit. "Yeah," he said, "can't blame you there." He stepped down off his horse, and gave the signal for his men to follow suit. "My name's Tuck, Joshua Tuck, Seventh Cavalry. We been after those three for a month now."

"Then you know about Lawrence and Clark?" Steele asked.

Tuck nodded. "Oh, yes. We been watching 'em. Seems to us they've been in on too many expeditions where the people all got wiped out by Indians. We sure want 'em for questioning, to say the least," he said with a sour grin. He pulled off his leather gauntlets. "They let Two Dogs do the dirty work."

"Tell us about it, Captain." Steele's voice was as dry as corn husk.

"You got taken by those two?"

"Sorry to say, we did. And they fought us twice. I think they'd have got what they wanted this time, if it hadn't been for you."

The captain was cooling off. "Well, I guess we did help there."

"We'd have been dead, sir."

Steele was very polite, suspecting what was coming next. He was right.

"You'll have to move out of here," the captain informed him.

"You mean to Deadwood?"

"No whites allowed in the Black Hills. Sorry."

"Captain, will you accompany me, sir? I want to see what the damage is."

"Maybe I can help," the captain replied.

Steele found that two had been killed, and several wounded. The dead men were married, and their wives were grieving. Steele did what he could to comfort them, and the captain ordered some medical supplies from his own stock for the wounded.

The buildings were blackened, and there was some charring, but they could be repaired. It would take work, but the people in Fort White were used to work, and the place would be habitable within a week.

That night there was a meeting.

Steele came right to the point. "The captain tells us we have to leave," he informed the group. "We are illegal here. No whites."

"I'm not leaving," a female voice declared. "Those rascals killed my husband, and I aim to stay, and mine gold just like he wanted."

"There's no place to go, anyway!" Jacobs shouted.

"Deadwood," replied the captain.

"Deadwood couldn't handle us. Town's full. Where would we stay?" said Jacobs.

It was a fair question, and the captain considered it. Laramie was too far. Deadwood was, after all, a boom town right now, and likely there wouldn't be extra room for twenty-five people.

"All right," the captain finally said. "I see

your point, but I do have my orders. No whites are allowed in these hills. Still," he shrugged, "sometimes the rules are bent a bit, and truthfully, I don't know just where the negotiations between the government and the Indians are right now. So," he continued, spreading his fingers on a makeshift table, "let me put it like this. If the situation is the same in the spring, you'll have to leave. Tomorrow, I'll give an escort to those who want to go back to Deadwood. Maybe some of you have had enough. Give me your answers in the morning."

The following morning, nobody showed up to accept the invitation. As he mounted his horse to leave, Captain Joshua Tuck grinned down at Steele. "I didn't think anybody would come. But," he added, "orders are still orders, and, if nothing changes, you'll have to move in the spring. Sorry. If I come back through, I'll move you out myself."

"I know." Steele grinned back. "Orders are orders."

The captain nodded, and left with his troops.

Later Steele found Elizabeth.

"Well," he said, "we can stay until spring, anyway."

"And then?"

"I'm going after Lawrence and Clark."

"So am I."

"But don't you want to mine?"

"First things first, Steele." Elizabeth's eyes were shadowed by anger. "I want to see the killers of my father—and these other men— brought to justice."

"You use such quaint talk."

"You know what I mean. I want to see them hung or shot."

"Yes. I know."

"But what about the rest of our group—do you think they'll leave?"

"Who, this bunch?" Steele laughed softly. "It'll take a lot more than cavalry—or Indians— to drive them out of Fort White. This is home now. Their blood and their graves are here, and those are ties that bind."

Elizabeth smiled, and her shadowed eyes lit with pride.

"We did all right, didn't we!"

"Just fine," said Steele. "Just fine."

And he looked at Elizabeth, and wondered if he was falling in love. He had never been in love, but at that moment the strangest feeling warmed his heart, and he felt very protective of Miss Elizabeth White.

Chapter Eight

The winter of 1876 passed too slowly for Steele. There was plenty to do. Wood, and lots of it, had to be brought in to keep the fires burning. Fresh meat was hunted daily in the hills, and hard-rock prospecting went on, except when the weather grew extremely cold. Both men and women learned to fashion clothing from warm furs and skins.

But underneath this layer of activity, there lay dormant in Steele one great desire—his mission—to get Pat Lawrence and Red Clark. He was infuriated to know they were at large, pulling their treachery on innocents. He didn't know just what he wanted from his mission— to personally challenge the pair, or to just bring them to justice. Circumstances, when they met, would settle that question. And they *would* meet.

Elizabeth was as determined, but Steele tried to discourage her.

"It will be dangerous," he said.

"I have faced danger," she reminded him.

"It will be tiring," he pointed out, "and dirty."

"I traveled by wagon train to this point," she said, "and if you don't think that was tiring and dirty, you are wrong."

"I can handle them," Steele insisted.

"I'm sure you can," Elizabeth said, "but, remember, it was my father who was killed, and I want to do something about it."

"I travel better alone."

"So do I."

"Now, look here—!"

"No," Elizabeth interrupted, "*you* look here. I'm going after those two, whether you like it or not. I don't have to answer to you. I'd rather go with you, because I think two can do more, but I'll go alone if necessary."

Steele gave in, but he was grumpy. "All right," he muttered. "Stubborn female."

Elizabeth smiled at him, despite the seriousness of the moment. "You're learning," she said.

In April, Steele resigned his post as leader of the Candy Mountain contingency. There were protests.

"You understand the country better than we do," Jacobs said.

"You know about mining, too," Crisp added, with a wry grin. "We're liable to wash out the gold and keep the rocks."

"And when it comes to Indians you got more savvy," said another.

Steele thanked them all.

"You people are veterans of two Indian fights, and you survived. That's as many as I've had, so you know as much as I do." He didn't mention his run-in with Two Dogs the year before. "Mining will come to you. You might pick up a few rocks, a bit of fool's gold, sure, but you'll catch on. As for knowing the country—yes, I'm a westerner, but you know *this* land as well as I, and this section is what you have to develop."

"How about supplies?" asked one of the women. "We have no guide."

"You still have plenty of food, because Lawrence and Clark brought more on their trip out." The irony escaped no one. "But if you need to get to Deadwood, catch on to some trapper or prospector coming through, and he'll take you in. Follow the rivers downstream, and you'll find a settlement. Don't worry about that."

Crisp turned to Elizabeth. "Are you going too?" he asked.

The girl pursed her lips, nodded, but said nothing.

"Well," Crisp said. "I think we'd all like to have a hand in catching those two murderers. I'll go."

Others joined in. There wasn't a man or woman who didn't want to see Lawrence and Clark hang.

Steele shook his head. "Too many would give us away. Two are enough. Maybe too many even then."

Elizabeth shook her head. She was going.

"Well." Crisp nodded toward the hills. "You

both better take out claims before you leave. We are finding good color, and, who knows? We might strike it rich—or at least pay for our time."

Steele and Elizabeth agreed, and after prospecting the land briefly, placed several claims.

After that they began packing for their journey.

"It's finally time," said Steele.

"Past time," Elizabeth agreed.

"You can still change your mind. It's safe here."

"Who wants to be safe?"

"Well," Steele hesitated. "Frankly, I'll worry about you."

"Well, Mr. Steele." Elizabeth smiled. "Do you think that much of me?"

"Well, Great Scott, can't you tell?"

"Where I've been concerned, Mr. Steele, you have been like a stone."

He thought about that, and realized the truth in her statement. He was in love with her, yet he'd never told her. He'd been busy on a day-to-day basis, keeping Fort White together, and his mind was filled with thoughts of Lawrence and Clark. Yet, he felt her presence always, and looked for her first thing each day. They didn't speak of such things as love, but the way he felt, he didn't think talk was necessary. For some stupid reason, he thought that his feelings showed. Apparently, he'd kept them a very good secret.

"Well," he said, "I haven't meant to be stone."

"You have."

"Look at it this way, will you? I love you."

Elizabeth laughed outright. "How thoughtful."

"I'm serious."

"Oh, I don't doubt it, but you could be a bit more . . . well, romantic. I'm not a horse, you know."

Steele was surprised. He thought he had been romantic—he checked on her every day, they had long talks about the fort, the weather, Lawrence and Clark, but, he suddenly realized, never about themselves. Still, shouldn't she know? "Can't you see my feelings in my attention, my eyes?" he asked her.

"Steele, Steele," Elizabeth said, shaking her head. "A woman wants more than signs. I want to hear you tell me, 'I love you.' I want to hear that love in your voice."

In the manner typical of him, he took direct action. Steele turned to face her, and she watched him with excited yet uncertain eyes. Then he leaned over and kissed her. Elizabeth stepped back, startled, then she kissed him back. He held her to him tightly, his strong arms around her slim waist. "Look, I know I'm not your idea of a romantic, maybe, but I sure haven't meant to hide what I feel," Steele said.

"I know." Elizabeth looked up at him. "Maybe I knew how you felt but I just wanted to hear you say it."

"Say what?" Steele was still dense.

"I love you."

"I just did a minute ago."

"I want it again, and I want to hear those words often. Women are funny about that. They like to be told they are loved every now and then," Elizabeth said.

She tucked her head back in his chest, feeling the warmth and the strength of his heart.

"Oh, pity," he grumbled, and she glanced up to see him smiling. He kissed her again. At that moment Crisp and Jacobs entered.

"Well, finally," Crisp said "We wondered if you'd ever get around to it, man."

"What do you mean?" Steele asked.

"The whole danged camp knew you were mooning over the girl. Some of the women were ready to stick you with their darning needles to prod you along!" He laughed. "Danged near prodded you myself." He looked at Elizabeth. "You are getting a good man."

"He is getting a good woman," she replied.

Both Crisp and Jacobs nodded at that. "One of the best," said Jacobs. "When is the wedding?"

"I don't know," Elizabeth said.

Jacobs looked at Steele. "Elizabeth and I have a job to do first," he replied. "We haven't had time to think of setting dates for weddings. I think when our job is over, we will return to Fort White and be married." He turned to Elizabeth. "What do you think of that?"

"We will be the first to get married in Fort White!" Elizabeth said happily. "My father would have liked that."

"You can still stay here," Steele said. "Where you'll be safe."

"Nope. You ain't gittin' away, cowboy, you don bin roped," she said in her best western accent.

They rode the next day, with Fuzz, Elizabeth's horse, Charlie, and a packhorse with supplies. They decided to visit Deadwood first.

"I don't think we'll find our men there, because Captain Tuck will be looking there, too," Steele said. "But it's a place to start."

Following his own advice, Steele hooked up with a traveling prospector, who led them to Deadwood in ten days. He was not surprised to learn that neither Lawrence nor Clark had been seen all winter.

"Army's after them scamps," he was told by one villager.

"The Army is not alone," Elizabeth said, and told the story of Candy Mountain. "There could be others like Clark around," she finished. "Let newcomers beware."

"Where should we go next?" Elizabeth asked. "Laramie, maybe?"

"Maybe, but I think white man's country might be too hot for them now." Steele said. "My bet is they are living with Indians."

"So what does that mean?"

"We have to find Indians."

"Is that safe?"

"No. You better stay here."

"Not on your life, cowboy."

But, first, they needed a rest and a cleanup—and a good meal. So they delayed a couple of days, washed the alkali dust out of their clothes and hair, and ate something besides bannock and beans.

There was no hurry. This was big country. Big country seemed to allow for time. Only the seasons urged the tempo along, and spring was in full swing now. The air was warm, the sun bright, and the blue sky huge and clear. The tempo of the moment was not fast; it was easy and low-key. Except for their inner anxiety, the urge to apprehend the two they sought, there was no reason to push.

Besides, Steele admitted, they didn't really know where to go—so why hurry there? Haste, he reasoned, makes waste. As much as he wanted to find Lawrence and Clark, he held on to his patience. Both he and Elizabeth enjoyed two full days in Deadwood.

At the end of two days, they left. Fuzz, never one to let good feelings go by without showing them, kicked up his heels, nearly throwing his rider.

Steele, recovering his balance, patted the feisty animal's neck.

"Easy, hoss," he advised. "You got a long way to go, yet."

Fuzz arched his neck and gave Steele a look, which amused Elizabeth.

"Do you two always communicate that way?"

"Always," Steele replied. "We talk a lot. You should try it with Charlie."

"He only mumbles," she replied with a smile. "I can't understand half what he says."

They departed Deadwood in good spirits, in spite of the somber undertones of their mission.

"I have the feeling," Elizabeth said, "that something good is going to happen."

"Of course."

The third day out of Deadwood, Two Dogs and his band galloped up and pointed an array of weapons at them.

"This is good?" Steele muttered.

"You come," the Indian chief invited. There

was nothing that the two whites could do except honor the invitation.

Their weapons were confiscated, and they rode to a camp on a nameless creek. They were thrust into a teepee, and a guard placed at the door.

"If the two we want are here, Two Dogs is not talking," Steele said.

He no sooner uttered the words than the guard ushered them out. Two Dogs was waiting. He had two knives, and gave one to Steele.

"We fight till one die," he said. He grinned. "You die, and I take her." He jabbed his knife at Elizabeth. "I give you a chance. You are good man, I think."

"Thanks, I appreciate your thoughtfulness," Steele responded dryly. "And if I win, will your braves let us free?" he asked.

"You have my word, you will both go." He looked at Elizabeth again. "Nice white squaw."

Elizabeth, shuddered. She had a knife hidden deep within her clothing. If Steele were killed, she would turn the knife on herself. Her life was with Steele, now. If he died, so would she.

Two Dogs lunged, and Steele dodged. The fight of his life was on.

Chapter Nine

Steele had one thing, in his favor—he was much heavier than Two Dogs. Because of his weight, he was able to pull his adversary off balance through sheer strength.

If not for that, he would have been dead in the first ten seconds. Two Dogs, lithe, and experienced in knife fighting, knew the tricks. He knew how to close, how to slice, and when to thrust, but Steele wouldn't give him the opportunity.

The dust billowed under the combatants' feet. Steele in the Texas boots, Two Dogs in moccasins, one clumping the ground clumsily, the other soft-footed, gliding, snakelike in grace.

A dozen times they stood chest to chest,

sweat gleaming from bared torsos, knives locked, every muscle trembling with the pressure.

Elizabeth shouted encouragement from the sidelines, where she was closely watching by two braves. Other Cheyenne watched, urging their chief on. This was not only a battle for life, but to preserve the tribe's pride. The whites were beating them on all fronts, and a victory here, though small, was important.

But Two Dogs realized early on that he had no easy opponent. Steele used his strength to his advantage—clumsy as it might be. Also, the white man was fearless, and he had endurance. The Indian chief admired how Steele showed no fear.

The two fought under the yellow sun for an hour, and red blood drenched their wrists from the thongs that bound them. The two battled silently, each intent on his opponent. The only sounds came from the onlookers.

Of the two, Two Dogs had the greatest endurance. Though Steele's superior weight and strength carried him well, the Indian's lithe body carried nothing extra. He was as hard as granite, and could last forever. Two Dogs had slept on little more than the hard ground all of his life. He withstood freezing temperatures with little clothing, save in extremes when furs were worn. The life he led in the extremes of the wilderness could yield only one result—an endurance equaled by no white man.

After a while, a gleam of triumph came to Two Dogs' eyes. He knew he had the white man, despite the other's strength. It would be only a matter of time. But into this certainly there came the shock of his life.

Steele knew exactly what the other was thinking, and realized something drastic would have to be done soon. A plan raced through his mind, and he flung it into action. With a giant twist of his tied wrist, Steele suddenly flung his adversary to the ground. He was on him in a flash, sitting on the lean, bony chest, his knife on his brown neck.

"One move, Two Dogs," said Steele in a husky voice, "and you die."

Two Dogs spat upwards into Steele's face. Steele did not flinch. His leg pinned Two Dogs' knife arm, and no matter how the chief struggled, he could not free his arm.

"Do it," the chief ordered, his voice flat. "I am defeated. I would kill you. Do it!" Two Dogs arched his neck for a better target.

For a brief moment, Steele was tempted. If he let the Indian up, it was possible that Two Dogs' pride, having suffered a blow, would cause him to attack Steele again. A quick rifle shot, perhaps, to end the white man who had humiliated him? And Elizabeth, what about her? A quick killing of the Cheyenne chief would answer those questions, because Two Dogs had given his word. There would be freedom for him and Elizabeth.

But he hesitated. He couldn't bring himself to shove his knife into the exposed throat. Though he had won the fight fairly, and though Two Dogs would certainly have killed him, it felt like murder.

"Two Dogs," Steele said, "I am not after you. You are not one of those I wish to fight. You could have beaten me easily, but luck was mine." He shrugged. "It was meant to be," he went on, playing to the Indian's belief that fate governed lives. "I do not want your life. I am after the white renegades Lawrence and Clark.

They caused the deaths of this white woman's father, and my friends. As you would have done, I must avenge those deaths. The men I seek are greedy. They are traitors, men without honor. They deserve to die. You do not.

"There is the big war you spoke of. Is it not important that you live for that?"

Then he cut the bonds that held their wrists, and leaped up quickly. He waited. Would Two Dogs order his men to shoot him? Would he come at him with his knife?

The Indian chief drew himself up. He studied Steele with his unreadable eyes. His warriors waited in a circle around them. One command, one gesture, and it would be over for him and Elizabeth.

After several moments, Two Dogs' eyes flickered. He said something to his tribesmen in their tongue, then turned to Steele.

"It is good you reminded me of the big fight to come." He nodded. "Yes, I have a larger duty than killing you. Soon, the Plains Indians will be free of the white man, and I will be useful in that battle."

"You could have killed me easily," Steele said. "But you let me live. Why?"

The Indian studied him, then said, "You are a good man. Yes, I could have killed you, but I wanted to play with you first, as the mountain lion does the ground squirrel."

That brought a murmur of appreciation from the other Indians.

Steele asked, "The white women and I can go now?"

Two Dogs shrugged. "The game is over. Yes. Go."

"I would like to ask one question. If you know where the whites I seek are, will you tell me?"

Steele wasn't sure he'd get an answer.

The chief hesitated, then said, "You might find them over at what you call the Little Big Horn River. We call it Greasy Grass. That is where many of my people are now. Maybe they are trading there. I do not know."

Steele nodded and glanced at Elizabeth. They needed to leave quickly, before some of the younger braves decided to test the white man. They found their horses and galloped off. After riding ten miles they came to the Rosebud River. Steele stopped to wash his wounds, while the horses drank. Elizabeth filled their canteens.

As Elizabeth dressed Steele's wounds she asked, "What big battle is coming?"

"I don't know, but for Two Dogs to speak openly about it means he is pretty sure of victory."

"Shouldn't we warn the Army?"

"I'd guess they have had warnings already. I don't think what we have to say will make a dent. No. We have our own game to play."

They continued, after watering the horses. That night they camped by a river, and during the dark hours heard noises. They did not make a fire.

The next day, they spotted a party of what Steele thought were Sioux from their dress. The Sioux saw them, and fired shots, but they did not do more than that. The bullets whistled past harmlessly, as the two whites galloped for cover.

A half hour passed.

"Now what?" he wondered out loud.

"Wouldn't they have ordinarily come after us?" Elizabeth asked, worried. She kept a sharp eye out.

"Yes. Must be after bigger game, and don't want to waste ammunition."

"Do you think they are going to the battle Two Dogs spoke of?"

"It's possible."

They proceeded with caution up the river. Whenever they saw Indians, they hid. Whether they were seen or not they could only guess, but they were not challenged.

"Lot of them around," observed Elizabeth.

"Too many," Steele said. Because of the Indian threat, progress was slow, but, Steele reasoned, they weren't sure of their goals anyway. Better to hide than risk a scalping.

Early one morning, they heard a fusillade of shots upstream. The noise rolled across the sky like thunder. The two laid low in a thick growth of cottonwood trees along the river bank.

"Do you suppose this is the big war?" Elizabeth whispered.

"Sure sounds like it." Steele glared at Elizabeth. "*Now*," he said angrily, "is when I wish you were at Fort White."

"A little late for that," she said. "You're stuck with me."

"Humph."

"Is humph the best you can do?"

Steele glared, and was immediately brought out of his bad humor, by the amused smile on Elizabeth's face. In spite of the unknown dangers around them, she could still laugh. Now *there* was a woman! He kissed her and whispered, "Sorry, but not sorry." He gave her a hug. "Really glad you're here, but not glad, understand?"

"No."

"Well, humph, then," he replied, but his petulance had by that time dissolved into happy acceptance. Elizabeth was in her rightful place—with him—and he knew it.

The sounds of what was surely battle kept up for some time, then were followed by silence. After a few hours, the two ventured forth. Walking their horses, they headed toward the area where they heard the battle. Several times tribes of Indians rode by, and Steele and Elizabeth were forced to take cover. The Indians were laughing and speaking in a mixture of tribal tongues. They seemed in good spirits. Steele wondered if they were indulging in the happy moments of victory.

Eventually they arrived at the battle scene. The 7th Cavalry was holed up, and Steele and Elizabeth were stopped by nervous sentries.

"Git down off them horses," one ordered.

"Now," said a second, cocking his rifle.

"Whoa, partner," Steele said. "We are friends. What happened here?"

"Them danged Injuns surprised us, and we had to fight," the first sentry said. He nodded toward a group of men. "Come on, I'm taking you to Captain Tuck."

"Joshua Tuck?" Elizabeth asked.

"The same. Know him?"

"Some," she replied.

The captain wasn't surprised to see them.

"I knew you'd be looking for Lawrence and Clark," he said. "It's a good thing you didn't stumble in here this morning. Look." He swept his hand in a circular motion.

There were dead horses by the score, flattened by Indian lead. Under a canvas fly a dozen men were being tended to by doctors. And nearby, other men were digging graves.

"We were a thousand strong," Tuck said, shaking his head, "and yet they hit us. Never seen anything like it. We have over one hundred and fifty dead and wounded, and look at them horses!" Tuck shook his head again. "When we fired back at them, those red devils didn't run. That's what they usually do—hit and run—but not this time. They *fought* us." Tuck was grim. "They'd have wiped us out, I think, but we were too many for them this time."

"You head of this bunch?" Steele asked.

"Good grief no, boy," Tuck answered. "Me, a captain, heading a thousand men? General Crook is your man."

Steele told Tuck about Two Dogs' talk of a big war. "Do you think this is it?"

"Hard to say, but we do know the Indians, all Great Plains tribes up north here, are gathering someplace. They used to meet at Bear Butte in the Black Hills, but there's too many whites for 'em there now, I guess. They meet out here someplace."

"How come you got a thousand men?" Steele was curious. "That's a lot of soldiers to be roaming around."

"To get the Indians back on their reservations. They are leaving by the hundreds and refuse to return."

"Maybe they don't like being cooped up."

The captain shrugged. "Maybe you are right, but that's not my worry. I follow orders—I'm in the Army, remember? And my orders are to put 'em back, where the government says they belong."

The captain glanced around, and bitterness darkened his eyes. "Only they ain't going peaceful. This isn't the last of the fight, I'm pretty sure."

"You see any white skins?"

The captain squinted in the sun. "Can't be sure—there was a lot of smoke and confusion. Maybe. Can't be sure." He shaded his eyes with his hand. "Going after those two is dangerous. Suicide maybe."

"I want them."

"So do I," Elizabeth added.

Tuck nodded. "We all do. Well, you're both crazy, but I think the Indians are heading for the Little Big Horn country."

"We heard that."

"Who told you?"

"Two Dogs."

"He must be pretty sure of himself to let it out—well, Custer is heading that way, too. The redskins will have their hands full with him."

"You mean old Long Hair is in on this?"

"Yep. Except he ain't Long Hair now. I hear his wife made him cut it." The captain laughed at what was apparently an inside joke.

Steele and Tuck shook hands.

"Good luck," Tuck said.

"Thanks for the talk," Steele replied. "What are you going to do now?"

"It's up to General Crook, but I hope, we go after those Indians," he said. "I want 'em for this. It's personal now. Good men died here."

Steele and Elizabeth headed north. He didn't like what he'd just seen. A force of Indians large enough to attack a sizable military contingent meant they had no fear of U.S. Army might. They were angry. Indians usually attacked in smaller groups, such as those who attacked Fort White. They struck and then ran. They were bold now. They meant business.

Elizabeth rode alongside of Steele, reflecting on what she saw. Steele noticed.

"Wasn't a pretty sight, was it?" he asked gently.

Elizabeth shivered. "There's more violence in the air. I can feel it."

"Keep that feeling. It makes you alert. You could save our lives."

They traveled at night to avoid the Indians, and the going was slow. Steele was no navigator. They had only the stars to guide them.

"I guess if we just keep to the left of the Big Dipper, we'll be all right," he said.

"Your guess is as good as mine. Lead on, John Fremont."

"I'm no explorer, Elizabeth."

"Maybe you aren't Fremont, but you're working blind just like he did, and he got to where he was going."

"Where was that?"

"He didn't know till he got there."

Steele looked at Elizabeth, and caught an impish gleam in her eyes. She teased him during the oddest moments!

"Have we had enough of teasing me?"

"Enough—for now."

"Is there no stopping you?"

"A kiss might work."

A kiss did work. He never knew he could care so much for somebody as he did Elizabeth White.

In spite of their caution, they met four Indians at dusk the third day after leaving the battle scene. The Indians approached swiftly, but Steele and Elizabeth cocked and pointed their rifles.

The Indians came to a stop, scowling, looking at the rifles with a mixture of fear and greed. Then one drew a finger across his throat.

"That sign means they are Sioux," Steele whispered.

"How do you know?"

"That's their greeting."

"Oh."

"Keep your rifle ready."

"Don't worry."

The four hostile Indians didn't move. They seemed to be sizing up Steele and Elizabeth. Then one yelled something, and they turned, their horses kicking up dust. Steele watched until they were specks.

"We will follow them," he said.

"They might be waiting."

"Maybe, but they most likely think we went in the opposite direction. Why would two whites follow four Indians?"

"That's a guess."

"Yes, but I think they were heading for something else—maybe Two Dogs' big fight. And I want to know what it is."

"Maybe Lawrence and his crooked friend will be there."

"We both hope for that."

They changed tactics, traveling by day. They needed to see the lay of the land now, and watch out for any suspicious signs. Steele picked up the trail of the four Indians, and they followed it cautiously. As they moved closer to the Little Big Horn River, they noticed more trails and hundreds of fresh horse tracks. There were also signs of lodge poles dragging.

"A very big camp is ahead someplace," Steele said. They reached the Little Big Horn, and followed it downstream. It was a muddy river, and the horses refused to drink from it, so it was necessary to reach clear, incoming streams.

The sun was very hot in the blue, opaque sky, and the air was thick with humidity. Heat waves danced across the rough hilly country, heavy, moisture-laden sheets that obscured distant vision like a faulty lens. The sense of violence was still in the air, only now, it was more intense than ever—as if an invisible monster crouched, ready to chew the world to pieces.

The oppressive heat, and the unpleasant sense that something big, and terrible, was going to happen, left Steele watchful, and a bit irritable.

They hadn't reached a fresh water inlet in half a day, and the horses were lagging.

"Why don't they drink muddy water?" Elizabeth wondered out loud.

"How should I know?" Steele snapped. He was immediately sorry. "I guess I'm feeling the mood of the country too well," he muttered.

"So am I," Elizabeth replied. "And I still wonder why horses won't drink muddy water."

"Because," Steele replied with a grin, his humor somewhat restored, "it's dirty. How's that?"

"Not good enough. If I were thirsty, I'd drink muddy water."

"You never give up do you!"

"No."

Steele grinned again. He leaned over and kissed her.

"Now," he said, "will you quiet down about why you can lead a horse to muddy water, but you can't make him drink?"

"I am afraid, Steele," she said suddenly.

He reached over and patted her hand. "So am I, if that is any help."

"Thanks for your assurance," she said dryly.

"It's free."

"It isn't worth any more than that, Steele."

On the tenth day after leaving the Rosebud, they saw smoke flattening in the sky some distance away. They dismounted their horses and led them toward the darkening sky.

They kept to the cottonwood trees that lined the river, traveling more cautiously than before. An hour later they first spotted the smoke. They rounded a bend, and saw an Indian village. It was more than a village, it was a city, a huge city of a thousand teepees, or more, and Steele was awestruck.

"There must be thousands of Indians," Elizabeth whispered.

Off to the right, on a large, flat plain, gently swept by very low, sloping hills, were thousands of horses. They were feeding on lush early-summer grasses.

"I think those are extra horses," said Steele. "Whatever is going to happen, the Indians must figure plenty of extra mounts will be needed."

"I wonder what it's all about?" Elizabeth was an Easterner, and had no idea what sizes Indian villages came in, but she intuitively realized that what they saw was far from the norm.

Suddenly a shot sounded in the muggy air. It came from downstream, below the giant camp. Another shot boomed, then several more, and then the air was bent with a solid wall of rifle fire. A blue column of United States Cavalry appeared to the left, across the river.

"Great Scott!" Steele shouted. "It's the beginning of a war! This is what Two Dogs has been talking about!"

Chapter Ten

"Must be more than one army group," Steele said. "The shots came from below the village, but the troopers we see aren't shooting."

Elizabeth was horrified and fascinated by what she was witnessing—an actual battle between the U.S. military and the Indians.

Their attention was riveted on the column of cavalry coming downhill across the river. In the lead was a buckskin-clad man, who began firing a pistol. All of the blue figures were firing now, and they charged swiftly, whooping and yelling.

Suddenly, a great host of mounted Indians charged up the hill to meet the uniformed men.

There was confusion as horses collided and men fell from their saddles, pierced by enemy arrows and lead. The Indians, far outnumbering the troopers, were in the midst of the blue line almost at once. The buckskin-clad figure fell from his horse, and others dismounted to form a ring around him. Still other soldiers urged their horses to higher ground. One by one, the men that circled the fallen man dropped from their own injuries. Some made a run for it, but they were shot down at once.

Blue powder smoke and dust, along with the dense heat waves, made visibility difficult, but Steele saw another contingent of mounted Indians attack from the upper side of the village. The Cavalry was trapped in a pincer movement. The enemy power was so great, that in spite of a valiant, desperate stand, the soldiers were simply overrun. Steele saw some put pistols to their own heads and pull the triggers— a sure death was better than capture. The Indians raced through the remaining blue-coated men, clubbing and tomahawking them, until there wasn't a soldier left alive.

Two Dogs retreated from the clamor of battle. The noise, the smoke of rifle fire, the screams of white soldiers were all music to his ears. This was what he had been waiting for: this day, this hour, was the result of many plans, many talks.

The Cheyenne chief had been wounded, his right arm slashed by a flashing knife. The wound was not dangerous, but bled too much. Two Dogs found a cloth and bound the injured flesh. He would survive. He grinned, for this wound would be a mark of honor he would bear for the rest of his life.

The chief had been in the first wave to attack the men in blue uniforms. He had charged on his war pony with a fierceness that filled his heart. The pony had been painted around the eyes, and an eagle's feather had been woven into his mane.

Two Dogs had also decorated his own body with war paint. Several feathers were in his hair signifying his status as a warrior. Among the Cheyenne, he was granted great respect, for it was known he had fought numerous battles in order to acquire more weapons. The fact that he had kept company with white men of evil reputation didn't matter. Weapons were his goal and he had fullfilled his promise.

His first taste of real battle had come a few days before when he and his band met soldiers at what the whites called the Rosebud River. Hundreds of warriors tried to wipe out the soldiers then, but there were too many soldiers, and the fight had been called off.

There was another fight coming, and the Indian braves were saving their ammunition for this one. This battle would be with Yellow Hair on the Little Big Horn River. It would be for justice.

Yellow Hair, known among his own kind as General Custer, had won a victory over Cheyennes at Washita River. The soldiers attacked on a winter day when the villagers were huddled in their teepees for warmth. By the time it was over, a hundred Indian men, women, and children had been killed. On top of that, 800 ponies were deliberately destroyed.

Custer, it was said, had been pleased by his victory.

It was thought by Two Dogs to be a cowardly attack. Other leaders were of the same opinion.

Two Dogs and chiefs of other tribes held meetings to discuss the matter. One thing was becoming very plain: the whites were growing in number at a very high rate. Indians of every nation were losing ground. There would have to be a stand someplace, at some time and soon. If a stand was not made, the Indian way of life would be lost forever.

It was agreed among the chiefs, and the warriors as a whole, that modern weapons were mandatory. True, every Indian was adept in the use of bow and arrows, the knife and spear. Past battles with whites, and, for that matter, inter-tribal quarrels, had proven that skill. But wise heads knew that rifles and pistols would be necessary in order to win. Repeating rifles, capable of holding many shots in their magazines, would give the Indians an edge. There were some rifles, and many muskets, but muskets were too slow in reloading. While a warrior was reloading, he could be shot dead seven times over.

Two Dogs and other chiefs started on a long pilgrimage. They became acquainted with dealers of weapons, who traveled the Great Plains selling their wares illegally. Whites were not allowed to sell firearms to Indians, who were considered hostiles, and a danger. But there was a dollar to be made in selling arms and there were unscrupulous men to take advantage of the idea.

And who, in a country so vast, was to discover them? The Great Plains stretched from the Dakotas south to Texas, and East to Indian Country, called Oklahoma by some. It was a simple matter to hide out, to await shipments from the East, and to sell the rifles where the demand arose. Sometimes the weapons came through battles with the whites, both travelers from the East, and soldiers stationed in western outposts. Sometimes, it was necessary to contact bloody men like Lawrence and Clark, who would sell their own kind for the skin of a weasel.

Two Dogs did not like dealing with the likes of Lawrence and Clark. They were dishonorable, and the Indian chief valued honor more than life itself. But he reasoned that the ends warranted the means. If Indians were to ever escape being overrun—no, *overwhelmed*—by the white race, many weapons were needed. And ammunition—tons of it. Tons.

Unaware that two whites were also watching the battle as it unfolded on the hill across the river, Two Dogs left his memories abruptly, and leaped on his pony. The horse, having drunk deeply from the river was ready, and he galloped forward—into carnage.

By now, the fight was nearly over. There wasn't a soldier left standing. Those still alive were quickly killed. Two Dogs himself ran his spear through two of them, who were struggling to fight back with raised pistols. The chief couldn't help but admire the fallen troopers. They had fought well, but were no match for the thousands of skilled warriors who ran over them like flood water in the spring.

The air was heavy with the stench of death. It was cloudy, too, with blue gun smoke that hung in the air. In the distance he heard more gunfire, and knew that another part of the Indian force was attacking more soldiers. Scouts had seen several companies that lagged behind Custer for some reason. The fact that the blue uniforms were not all together was disappointing. It had been planned to catch all the soldiers at the same time.

Two Dogs shrugged. He was sure the last shot would be fired in a little while.

The chief rode his pony slowly through the mass of bodies. He did not know how to count in the white man's way, but he realized there were many dead—what was called a "company" of men—at least that many, perhaps two companies.

He brought his mount to a stop beside a soldier with yellow hair: General Custer. He noted two things: the hair was not long, it had been cut short, and there was a hole in Custer's temple. Had he been shot and instantly killed? Or had he turned his weapon on himself? Several soldiers had done so during the battle. Suicide was better than capture, because prisoners were often tortured to death.

Yellow Hair's body would not be mutilated, because the Indians believed that a suicide should not be scalped or the body be harmed.

But the warriors were taking the spoils of war—weapons were pried from dead, clutching hands. Clothing was stripped from bodies, jewelry admired and put into pouches for later examination.

The warriors gave way to the women coming from the temporary village of a thousand tee-pees. Steele and Elizabeth saw what the women did to the bodies, and she would wonder about that for the rest of her days.

Two Dogs lingered yet awhile. He continued to guide his pony carefully among the corpses. He also helped to tend to his own wounded and dead. There were many, but not so many as had been anticipated by the chiefs. This was partly due to the rifles of the troopers. The brass shells had swollen in the breeches after being fired. The ejecter systems were not working properly, and failed to eject the shells. This meant that troopers were forced to dig the exploded shell out with sheath knives, before levering another shell into the breech. Such a loss of time cost lives.

Still, the loss of Indian life was signficant, and there were many wounded. The bodies were carried off, and the wounded were either carried or they managed to limp back to the village. The wounded would be cared for by the shaman or medicine man. The dead would be carted back to home grounds, or disposed of in ways that were honorable.

The sound of rifle fire was still heavy to the south. Great bands of warriors had gathered on the flatlands across the river. They charged into the hills, disappearing in the gullies, but after unloading their rifles converged on the flatlands again. Two Dogs could not see the troopers, who were well hidden in the hills, but he could see the warriors. They seemed to be debating, but were too distant to be heard.

The main leader of the Indians, Sitting Bull, a Hunkpapa Sioux, was conferring with other chiefs. Sitting Bull was a veteran in resisting white enchroachment. He had fought many battles and was feared among the whites, both civilians and soldiers. One of the reasons for his leadership now was his experience and wisdom.

Two Dogs admired Sitting Bull. He had sat in council with him once and realized he was in the presence of greatness. The man spoke without hesitation, knowing what must be said and how to say it.

He was an orator of significance. He was a natural leader.

For a moment, Two Dogs thought about joining the battle to the south. He was curious. What was going on? The fighting should have ended by now. But as he hesitated, his arm began to throb, and he felt a flow of fire in his viens. He knew the signs of fever, and decided to return to the village for treatment. A warrior in fever is not the best man for the job. If the fighting continued tomorrow, he would join the others.

Two Dogs was not married. His wife had died of a mysterious illness during which her skin became splotchy, and covered with scabs. There had been no children, and before his wife died, they had considered taking the children of others who had been killed in the battle against whites, or from other causes. After his wife's death, he remained childless and single— though there was a maid among his people whom he had seen glancing at him.

He was, after all, still young and a good hunter—a plus, he liked to think, in any maiden's life.

A shaman wrapped his injured arm in a blanket of herbs, and advised him to lie down awhile—advice Two Dogs was happy to take. He was really feeling low by now. If the fight went badly to the south, and help was needed, he would join at once, of course. But others were leaving battle, too. Night was coming and with it a cease fire. Scouts would be posted, but actual battle would ease up.

Two Dogs returned to his teepee, where he scarfed down some pemmican. Then he lay on some buffalo robes, and let his mind slip into a semi-consciousness. He could hear everything, but the will to move was taken from him. It was as if he were in a state of suspended animation.

The sun flamed the sky for a few minutes, then sank out of sight, beneath the flat of the western prairie. The camp came to a strange sort of life, a mixture of grief and triumph. In his haze, Two Dogs knew what was happening: the dead were being mourned; the great victory of the day was being heralded. Even though there was still danger to the south, the enemy had been cowed, Yellow Hair slain.

It was not often that Two Dogs allowed himself to daydream. He was a realist, a man who took life at face value. Once, as a boy, he had played a game with another boy. He had been given a bow and several arrows by his father. The other boy had received the same from his own father. They decided to stalk each other, the object to shoot arrows so close the other would surrender.

Two Dogs' aim was good, but not that good, and he hit the other boy in the shoulder, seriously wounding him. The other boy lived, and was, in fact, a part of the war right now, but Two Dogs never played such games again.

"Life is real enough without games," he told his wife during their first days together.

He missed his wife. He talked to her. They shared a closeness that fit them both well. Perhaps the maiden who glanced at him? Perhaps.

As the noise of celebration and grief drew in on him, he knew he should join the others. He was, after all, a large part of the leadership. So, even in a state of delirium, he left his shelter and did his best to join in. He was embarrassed that a white man's knife had so injured him, and he refused to talk about it to sympathetic friends.

But, in the end, he retreated to his quarters, and lay down on the robes. And then he allowed himself to daydream. These thoughts had been in his mind for a long time, long before today. Was he being realistic to allow them? Maybe not . . . but. . . .

He allowed himself to think about Sitting Bull. Here was a man capable of bringing together thousands of warriors and their families. He had the force needed to start a war for freedom—that was how he, Two Dogs, thought about it if Sitting Bull didn't put the idea into so many words. Freedom! Free to be one's own man, without the degrading influence of white men!

Two Dogs' people, the Cheyenne, were not originally of the Great Plains. They were from the northern region of great lakes, and were farmers. Gradually, they migrated to the West, invading Sioux territory. They ran into trouble with the Sioux, who dominated that part of the region. The Sioux were fierce adversaries, protectors of their land, but the Cheyenne were

as brave, and there were many bloody skir-
mishes.

There came a time when both peoples realized that they were involved in a no-win situation. Just before the white man began
invasions in large numbers, the two tribes
made peace. They shared customs and both
factions also shared a hatred of whites. The
Cheyenne men averaged a height of six feet,
the tallest of the Plains Indians. They were for-
midable in battle, and joined forces with any
who thought as they did about the advance of
the bluecoats.

As Two Dogs lay on his buffalo hide bed, he
thought about these matters, as they had come
down to him through storytelling of the elders.
They had grown strong and the warriors were
brave, and they were always determined that
the whites were not going to drive them out—
or put them on reservations. Two Dogs knew
about them, and he shuddered. To be stuck on
a reservation was to be jailed. No freedom. He
and his fellow tribesmen would be less than
alive.

Was the battle going on now a sign? There

would be payback from the military. Every Indian involved was sure of that. There were many soldiers who were skilled in the ways of war. They had been involved in their own great war not long before, and were as fearless as any warrior on the Plains. Once a man faced enemy fire, and returned it, he was never the same man again. He was to be watched and carefully assessed.

Could the tribes stand up to the deadly experience of the white man?

This was the time for the Indians to test themselves. This was the time, Two Dogs sat up straight when the thought hit him, to form a nation of their own! It would be a real nation of combined tribes, with borders, and an army to protect it.

Two Dogs gasped. The idea was daring, and original. At least he'd never heard it spoken aloud. To form one's own country! And why not? This gathering of thousands of natives proved that they could unite. If they acted quickly, before more thousands of soldiers gathered, couldn't the Indians post their new borders, and defend them?

The time to plan was now, right now, before the tribes vanished after the present fight.

Sitting Bull, whom everybody respected, would be the leader. As an orator of power he would have great influence, but other leaders were present as well. There were also Crazy Horse, Gall, Fast Bull, and Black Moon, to name only a few; all were present, and all had the respect of their followers.

Nor did the leaders need to stop with only Plains tribes. The Apaches to the south were white resisters, and those tribes by the great shining water toward the sunset, the Duwamish, the S'Kallams, and others might be interested. Why not? All were, or would be soon, dominated by the white race.

So thinking, dreaming thus, Two Dogs drifted into a deep sleep. His wound, the fierce actions of the day, had wearied him more than he realized. He slept until dawn, when noise in the village woke him.

He ate more pemmican, went to the river and drank the murky water. He washed his wound, then retrieved his horse from the tethering place where hundreds of other horses circled nervously. Excitement was in the air, and the animals sensed it in their human masters.

Mounting his pony, Two Dogs joined other warriors, and took over a position of leadership as a war chief. He led them toward the sound of rifle fire once again echoing in the small, rolling hills across the river.

He approached cautiously, and for the first time saw what was happening. The troopers had dug in at the top of a hill close to the river. Well protected by earthen embankments, the warriors dared not rush the bluecoats. They could be picked off easily. The battle had settled into a desultory scattered firearms duel in which neither side was making headway.

This was quite different from yesterday's quick decisive battle. At that time thousands of warriors had simply overrun the enemy. Today, the native force was stopped by the protective steep hill the soldiers had transformed into a fort. If a brave showed himself, he was killed or wounded. Nor could fire be returned easily, since the targets were well hidden from view.

It was a stalemate.

Two Dogs toured the area, keeping well hidden in thick trees that lined the banks of the Little Big Horn—that same forest that hid Steele and Elizabeth upstream.

Though he found no Indian bodies, he did see several soldiers in death. They had apparently been caught when racing for the cover of the hills. They had not yet been mutilated, for it was too dangerous. The bodies were in full view of the fortress on the hill. To disturb the dead soldiers could open the doors of death to would-be plunderers or mutilators.

As Two Dogs surveyed the scene, his warriors decided to join the fight on the hill as best they could. He led the way across the river, but in crossing lost two men and two horses. One of the lead chiefs, probably Black Moon, ordered them back.

We will wait till darkness, came the word. *We cannot dislodge the bluecoats in daylight.*

Two Dogs saw to it that his dead warriors were taken back to the village, but was left brooding. He had made a mistake allowing his men to cross the open river. That was bad for him, and he didn't like the feeling. He would have to take a dare to show his bravery and retain his respect.

One of the soldiers lay in an open patch of the forest. It was exposed to the gunfire from the hill. Dangerous. In an instant Two Dogs made up his mind. Leaving his pony in the forest, he walked to the open space. His friends and the chiefs called to him to get back, but he ignored them. He felt this was something he had to do: he would count coup. Touching the dead soldier was a mark of bravery since the act would take place under fire.

He walked slowly across the clearing, and knelt beside the dead man. He touched him with his hand, and the first bullet whistled by. Two Dogs did not hurry. He deftly peeled the blue tunic from the body, and as he did so more bullets ripped past. Slowly, as if there were no more hurry than going for a drink of water, he walked back to the protection of the forest.

He had not been touched. Forever after, one of his tribal names would be, "He Who Scorned Death," a mark of great respect.

The fight continued the rest of that day.

Many of the younger braves wanted to rush the hilltop, and gain victory, but the big chiefs were against the tactic. Too many warriors would be lost.

Two Dogs sensed a lessening of war-drive, too. The chiefs were talking among themselves, their faces lined and serious. Two Dogs joined in the talk, as was his right as a war chief. Black Moon, and Fast Bull were in favor of pulling out. Sitting Bull was not present, so his voice was not heard. Gall and Crazy Horse were uncertain. The issue would be settled when night covered the land once again, and the fighting ceased.

His wound was still bothering him, so Two Dogs went to his teepee on returning to the village. The two warriors who had been killed in the attempt to cross the river lay in state near their own teepees. Two Dogs visited the bodies and talked to the families before returning to his home. Plans for a ceremony were on hold. There seemed to be a hesitancy in the village, coupled with a tangible restlessness. It was as if noone knew quite what to do.

Back on his buffalo hides, Two Dogs consumed some more pemmican, but he did that from a sense of duty to his body, more than from hunger. He might be called on at any time to resume the fight, or, as he was beginning to suspect, break up camp.

Once again, his thoughts traveled to the evening before. *My mind is a rabbit,* he grunted, *traveling in circles in search of food.*

Would it be possible to establish an Indian nation? He had heard of the Great White Father back in the mysterious East. That man was the leader of the whites, and apparently a strong person—otherwise how did he get so many to come into this country? He must have great power to order soldiers into hostile country.

That was the kind of leadership needed now, the kind of leadership that could form a nation—and then protect it. Sitting Bull was that leader. Possibly Crazy Horse could do it. He had a big following among the Sioux. He was a challenging figure, with blue eyes, a rarity among Indians, and a commanding reputation as a fighter.

Or one of the other leaders might fit the category. Gall, Fast Bull, or Black Moon? They were present now because of their reputations as fighters. Fighters would be the key ingredient. Two Dogs had traveled enough during his search for weapons that he knew about the power of the whites first hand. He had visited the forts of the white man, and the villages, and saw their determination to establish themselves. Such a people would be difficult to dislodge.

But was dislodging necessary? The point of a new nation would be to establish native populations, the Indians, not to dislodge people. Once boundaries of a new Indian nation were established, let the whites have their forts and villages, but let Indians have theirs as well.

Feeling better after eating, and some rest, Two Dogs left his lodge. He would find Sitting Bull, and confer with him. He would assemble all the chiefs, and, for that matter, as many warriors that wished to attend. The Indian way was open in matters of this kind. Everyone could attend who wished.

Sitting Bull's lodge was across the other side of the village. It was a large teepee, housing his immediate family, and made from soft-tanned buffalo hides.

But the great man was gone. He, and his immediate followers, his personal council, had decided to retreat across the borders into the country known as Canada.

Two Dogs was dismayed. The battle had been won, so why desert now? Victory was in hand. Now was the time to push for more; now was the time to establish a new nation.

He found Black Moon and put the question in his troubled mind to the chief.

"The reason for our departure," he was told, "is that a white general is near with many troops. We cannot stay here."

"But we can beat them again. We are of large numbers"

"True, but we cannot last. The whites are without number. It is better to retreat for now. Perhaps later we can fight again and win."

The firing to the East had stopped, indicating that the braves had left the battle line. Two Dogs realized that whatever he might have said about a new nation would not make a point. The matter had been decided: it was time to break camp and return to home grounds. He regretted that he didn't have the chance to at least talk to Sitting Bull, or in more depth with Black Moon. The idea for an independent nation was good. It was, so far as Two Dogs was concerned, the only way to go.

Perhaps, sometime in the future he could bring it up again.

For now there was much to do and it would be done under the cover of darkness. In spite of the fact that there were thousands of people present, and thousands more horses, the undertaking was completed in an eerie silence. Teepees were dismantled, and folded; lodge poles were lashed together to form travois platforms. They were hitched to horses trained for the task and loaded. All goods were thus carried, plus the wounded and many of the dead. Some of the dead were left in their lodges, as they were they were too burdensome to carry far. But the lodges were designated as places of honor, and the dead would be remembered.

As the moon began to set a huge migration began. What took weeks to assemble vanished in a few hours. Various tribes took different routes to home grounds. Some would retreat to the Black Hills, others more north toward Canada, as had Sitting Bull. Each tribe would return to the place it knew best, a valley, a river, a region called home.

Two Dogs was among the last to leave. He had his travois in place and would help herding his tribe's horses to their own valley. He noted the maiden who had glanced at him was smiling his way. He smiled back. She was young but strong and willing. With her he would have many children and he would tell them stories of this great event.

While Two Dogs was thinking about a new nation, the two white people feared for their lives, as the massacre of the first day took place.

All at once, it was over. Steele reckoned that the massacre had taken less than fifteen minutes. A whole contingent of soldiers had been killed. They continued to watch the gruesome scene. Many Indians continued to scalp the bodies, while others stole the blue military coats. They were valued by warriors, as symbols of a victory over the hated white man.

"Good grief," Steele, murmured, filled with pity. "There must have been two hundred troopers in that cadre, and not one lived."

From below the village, below the scene of massacre, shots could still be heard, muffled in the thick, humid air. As Steele and Elizabeth listened, the sounds of battle could be followed, and they eventually ended on top of one of the hills, not far from the river. The battle did not move again.

"Whoever is leading that bunch has to stay put, or get wiped out," Steele said.

"How awful," Elizabeth whispered.

"Terrible," Steele said, and he took Elizabeth in his arms. They sat quietly, letting down their guard for the time not concerned that their horses might in some way betray their hiding place. For the time, they just didn't care. They were numb from what they just witnessed, and they retreated into a shell.

After some time, Steele broke the silence. "I wonder if we should go for help."

"Where would we go?"

Steele thought for a moment.

"You're right," he said. "There's nobody we can tell. Crook is too far away."

"Do you think we should join them on the hill?" Elizabeth asked.

Steele shook his head. "We are two guns more against many thousand. Besides, I don't think we'd get that far." He kissed her, then said, "I don't want to chance getting captured. I'd hate to think of what would happen to you. The squaws would have their fun." He shook his head rapidly, spooked by his own thoughts. "No, it's best we lay low."

"What if the Indians come looking for survivors and find us?"

"I don't think they'll do that. The Indians have had a big victory. They will be celebrating. And there is still the fight on the hill to keep them occupied."

Night came and the fighting ceased. At dawn, the shooting began once more. It intensified, then died down, then increased again.

"Somebody in command simply won't give up," Elizabeth said.

The fight continued all day. Occasionally, a drift of wind caused unpleasant odors from the massacre scene.

"At least we have water," Elizabeth said putting on as good a face as she could. "Even the horses are drinking it."

Both Fuzz and Charlie tucked their soft muzzles into the muddy river and drank tentatively.

"Just goes to show you—you do what you have to do, to keep your tonsils wet."

"Do horses have tonsils?"

"Yes, big as onions and twice as hot. That's why a horse drinks so much."

"Steele! How can you tease at a time like this?"

"If we are caught by the redskins, girl, this might be the last tease I'll get in the world. Thought I might as well get back at you."

Elizabeth snuggled against him. "A terrible thing has happened here."

"For the whites, but not the Indians. Listen."

Chanting and songs came from the village. A great battle had been won over the mighty white man. Now, perhaps, the whites would know that Indians were a power, too. Now, the Indians could keep their ground, and the Great White Father in Washington would honor treaties. It would be known that Indians were not afraid of war, not even against the Army.

Steele and Elizabeth remained in hiding. Shots continued on the hill across the river, but neither Steele nor Elizabeth could see the soldiers.

During the second night after the massacre noises were heard from the Indian village. The firing had ceased. Steele didn't dare move for a better look but strange things were happening.

Daylight on the third day brought a startling sight. Nearly all of the teepees were gone—vanished. Here and there a lone teepee stood, solitary, and somehow forbidding. Aside from those there was nothing but trampled grass and campfire remains. A frightening vast emptiness lay on the silent land, as if some black magic had swept away an entire world.

"I can't believe this," Steele said.

"Let's go see one up close," said Elizabeth. "Then we can believe."

Mounting Fuzz and Charlie, they cautiously approached the first silent teepee. Steele watched for Indians, ready to run.

"If this is some kind of trick, and the redskins return," he said, "head up there." He pointed to the hills across the river from which the shots had last come. "My bet is we'll find soldiers there—unless, they've been killed by now."

The teepee proved to be a burial place for a slain warrior. He was laid out on skins with his weapons. His wounds had been washed clean. The smell from the bloated body was nauseating.

"Let's get out of here," Steele said, gagging.

Out of curiosity, they peered into several more teepees and found the same.

"Enough of this," Steele said again.

Elizabeth agreed, but said, "What about those men on the hill?" She nodded toward the bodies of the troopers.

"Are you sure you want to go over there?"

"Do we have a choice? Some of those men might need help."

They crossed the Little Big Horn. The sun was high now and heat waves danced like long, moist spirits in the dense air.

The two approached the ghastly scene slowly. It was much worse than the burial tents. Men lay in grotesque postures, many naked, most cut up, freed of limbs and heads. All were swollen, and the stench was powerful. Elizabeth and Steele were both nauseated, and wore kerchiefs over their faces to block the odors. Elizabeth was crying.

"They didn't have a chance," he said quietly. "It was fifty to one, maybe more."

"Two Dogs' 'big war'?" Elizabeth asked.

"Most likely."

They dismounted next to the body of the man in buckskin.

"He was a colonel," Steele said.

"And he wasn't mutilated like the others," Elizabeth added.

"I think that's a mark of respect."

Elizabeth shuddered. "They kill a man and that's respect?"

"We live in a different world. How the Indians think—well that's a mystery to all except them."

Steele looked toward the hill from which they heard the most recent shooting.

"There's nothing we can do here," he said. "They're all dead. We better get over to the hill, and see what is going on."

"I'm afraid of what we'll find," Elizabeth said. "But I suppose you're right."

They rode cautiously, watching for Indians. They had traveled a couple of miles when a trooper rose suddenly from a hole he had dug in the rocky ground. He pointed a large rifle at them.

"What you doin' here?" he demanded. His voice cracked; he seemed dumbfounded.

"We just came from over there," Steele said pointing toward the massacre scene.

"Say," the soldier cried angrily, "what's goin' on there? How's come the colonel didn't give us a hand here? We been pinned down for two days."

"They are all dead," Steele said.

"What?" The soldier stared at them. "That's hard t' believe." He shook his head. "Dead? You some kind of idiot?" He hefted his rifle. "You better come with me."

The man led the way a quarter of a mile to a scene similar to what Steele and Elizabeth had seen at Rosebud River. Soldiers were dug into a hill. Wounded were resting, protected by the bald brow. Other troopers were cupped in round shallow holes, facing all directions. There were dead men under a canvas, and Steele spied unmoving blue uniforms farther down the hill.

An officer approached.

"Look what I found," said the sentry. "A couple of civilians—likely traders or camp followers or somethin'."

"I'm not a camp follower!" Elizabeth exclaimed, embarrassed.

The officer touched his cap. "That's easy to see, Miss." He nodded at the trooper. "Back to your post, Smith." The trooper left. "I'm Major Reno, commander of this contingent," the officer said. "What's with Custer? You must have seen him."

"All we know is that all of the men over those hills are dead," Steele told the major. "Was Custer dressed in buckskins?"

Reno nodded.

"Then he is dead, too. All were killed."

Reno called to another officer. "Captain Benteen, you hear that?"

"I heard," he replied, grimly. "We haven't dared move beyond the point where Smith was—too many Indians. What about them?"

"They are gone," Steele answered.

Benteen's face seemed to cave in, and for a moment, he didn't speak. Then he said to Reno, "It's over."

At that moment a bugle sounded in the distance. "That has to be General Terry's command," Reno said, nodding. "That's why the Indians are gone. They knew he was coming."

Benteen allowed a harsh laugh. "There was no need for them to stay. They did what they set out to do—beat us at our own game."

"We didn't know about Custer," muttered Reno. "We heard shots, but . . ." he drifted off. "We just didn't know. We thought they were still on their way."

"We better go meet, General Terry," the Captain decided, "I don't want to, but let's go by the scene of the massacre."

He and Captain Benteen saddled their mounts, and left, leaving Steele and Elizabeth without another word. The news of Custer's defeat had spread rapidly throughout the contingent of troopers, and there was a dreadful quiet. Steele nodded at Elizabeth, and the two returned to river. Along the way, they encountered more dead soldiers.

Elizabeth was pale. "Why, do men fight?" She suddenly burst out. "Is it their silly pride?"

"Hey," Steele reached over and touched Elizabeth gently, "I don't like this any better than you."

"I know, I know, Steele. Please go along with me, will you?" She asked. "I'll get over it, but it's so horrible, and, so futile. All of these men killed, and for what?"

"Well, for what it's worth, my opinion is the Indians are fighting for their land. They are losing it to whites, and they are doing what they can to hold it." He shook his head. "The sad part is, they can't win. Too many whites for them to beat."

Steele was quiet for a minute, considering their next mission. He was sure that Lawrence and Clark were with the Indians who would protect them.

"But what trail do we follow?" Steele swept his arm in a wide motion. "The Indians have left dozens of tracks, each tribe returning to its own land. Lawrence and Clark could be with any!"

"That," agreed Elizabeth, "is like looking for a needle in a haystack."

Chapter Eleven

Steele chose the largest trail, the one with most traffic.

"If we catch up," he told Elizabeth, "I think it's likely our boys will be with them. The more Indians, the more money."

"Let's be careful," she said nervously. "Remember, these people are dangerous."

"I'll never forget."

The Indians made no attempt to cover their tracks.

"The big victory has made them confident," Steele said. "They think they are indestructible."

"But they must know that General Terry is near," Elizabeth said.

"Yes, but they nearly whipped Crook, and they did whip Custer," Steele pointed out. "They are ready for another fight."

In spite of what must have been cumbersome luggage consisting of wounded braves, entire villages, the Indians made good time.

"They know the country," Steele acknowledged, "and exactly where they are heading."

They followed the most visible trail for three days without seeing any Indians. Plenty of signs, but no sign-makers. On the fourth day, they spied Two Dogs and his posse. They sat on their horses waiting.

Steele raised his hand, palm outwards, in a friendly greeting. At least he hoped the chief would take it as friendly.

"Didn't think we'd catch up to you," Steele said.

"You didn't catch up," replied Two Dogs. "I see you, and stop."

There were a dozen warriors in his party, none of them seeming to bear a friendly attitude.

"You see what we did at the river," Two Dogs continued. "Why follow us? We could kill you."

"We have no fight with you," Steele said. "I think you know who we want."

The chief nodded. "You don't give up easy, eh?"

"I'll never give up," Steele nodded toward Elizabeth. "Nor will she."

Two Dogs nodded, then spoke to his men in the Cheyenne language.

There was some lively talk, and it sounded threatening to Steele, but in the end, the young chief said, "You did not take my life when you could. I owe you." He pointed down the back trail. "You go back. Those two not with us like you think. They in the hills, I think, maybe city."

"In the Black Hills?"

Two Dogs spat in disgust. "We call those hills *paha sapa,* sacred to us. You go now." The chief's voice hardened. "This is our war year. We fight whites, show them we own land. We fight you, too, so go, while I hold my warriors back."

Steele touched his forehead in salute, and started to leave, Elizabeth close behind. Then Two Dogs started shouting.

"Those two you follow," he said, "I hope you kill them. They promise much, give little. They do get us things now, charge big price for them." Two Dogs spat again. "We have no use for them. They are traitors to us, and to their own kind. No honor."

With that lengthy speech over, the war chief whirled his horse and, followed by his men, left without a glance back.

Steele watched as the Indians departed. "So," he said quietly, "this is their war year."

"Meaning?"

"It means the Indians are going all out to keep their land. Custer's massacre and what happened to Crook on the Rosebud is just the beginning."

"They haven't a chance, Steele. We have too many guns. If they have one, we have a hundred."

Steele nodded in agreement. "Yes." His voice was soft. "But it is something they have to do—fight for their homes."

"Like we did at Fort White?"

"Like Fort White?"

"Do you think Two Dogs was lying to get us off Lawrence's trail?" Elizabeth asked.

"Did you watch his face?"

"I couldn't help but do that. He's so wild looking."

"We have to have faith in that look. It was the truth of hate."

"So what do we do, go to Deadwood after all?"

"No."

"I don't understand."

"Those two are dead men in Deadwood. With the Army looking for them, they wouldn't dare."

"Then where will we go?"

"Laramie, I'd guess. Knowing them, they are probably selling Candy Mountains to easterners right now—and they are a long way from Captain Tuck there."

"I wonder if any gold has been found on our Candy Mountain?" Elizabeth wondered.

"Well, there is gold in the area. And we did find colors. Maybe there'll be a strike." Steele shrugged. "I think we have more important things to think about, right?" He paused. "Anyway, I think we ought to share it—if we do find gold."

"What do you mean?"

"I mean, the ground isn't ours, really. It still belongs to the Indians. If we find gold, we should share with Two Dogs and his tribe."

"I like that."

"Thought you would." He leaned over and kissed her. "How was I ever so lucky to get you?"

"How was I?"

"Gee, I don't know. I ran till you caught me, I guess."

"Steele! Stop that!" But Elizabeth was laughing. "I love you," she said, "and that's no teasing matter."

"True." Steele kissed her again. "OK, enough of this mushy love stuff. We have a long way to go."

"I'm with you."

It was a two-week journey to Laramie over a dusty trail. The days seemed brighter, the sky bluer, the sparse, white clouds fluffier. The sagebrush smelled more pungent, the air was sweeter to breathe, and alone with all of these amenities, the crystal of hate was sparkling within Steele. Along with nature's best, the workings of anger strode.

He sensed that Elizabeth was going through the same personal paradox, enjoying nature, while at the same time nourishing a hatred that could end only two ways: death for her, or death for the two who had caused the murder of her father.

They reached Laramie at sundown, and rode the main street wearily, always on the look for Pat Lawrence and Red Clark.

"Suppose they aren't here?" Elizabeth was worried. "What then?"

"We start all over."

The town was alive with would-be miners— cowboys, easterners, mountain men, slick gambler types in suits and tall hats, and merchants. Black Hills was mentioned often, for more gold had been discovered.

Wagons lined upon the streets caught Steele's attention.

"Where there are wagons, there's apt to be the two people we want," he said, and then added, "I'm not wasting time, when we see those two. If anything goes wrong, and you live, head back to Fort White. Don't hang around trying for revenge. You'd never make it against those two."

"I'll make that decision myself," she replied coolly. Besides, nothing's going to go wrong."

Steele's face tightened. "Everything could go wrong. Two rifles could be pointed at our backs right now."

Elizabeth felt a chill in her lower back, and for the first time fear rode alongside hate. But it wasn't fear for herself. *If anything happens to him,* she vowed, *I'll even the score. I swear it.*

The two men they sought were in a bar celebrating a new coup.

"It ain't the Candy Mountain trick," Clark was saying, "but there's twenty thousand in it for us to split, more when we get the wagons back."

Pat Lawrence nodded with a satisfied smile. He stroked his long, false mustache, and straightened his shoulders, still looking every inch the frontiersman he liked to portray.

"There's only one thing," he said. "We have to find someone to replace Two Dogs."

"Yeah, after Custer, he don't need us. Hates us, I think. We got out of there just in time. But I think I got another Injun . . ."

Clark's words trailed off. Lawrence glanced up from his beer and noted his partner's eyes were glued on the swinging doors of the saloon. Lawrence followed Clark's staring eyes, and he, too, froze. Steele and Elizabeth were watching them.

Without hesitation, Lawrence went for his pistol, shouting, "There's the man who robbed us!"

Steele's own draw, smooth and fast, was nonetheless slower. Lawrence's gun was already out, and he shot. The bullet roared through the room, and men dodged behind anything available. It went wide missing its target. Steele aimed calmly as Lawrence fired again. Steele stood fast and sure, and then he squeezed the trigger. Lawrence crashed backward, the bullet making its mark where Steele wanted it—Lawrence's forehead.

Clark, stunned into inaction for a few seconds, drew his gun, and shot. Steele felt hot lead sting his arm. The jolt threw him back. Clark fired again, a savage grin lighting his face. He was sure he could finish off his injured quarry. But Elizabeth opened fire with her own weapon. The shot hit Clark, and the man stumbled backward, then crashed to the floor by another bullet from Steele.

Then there was quiet. Lawrence and Clark lay dead. Lawrence looked small, nothing like the gallant frontiersman he loved to portray in life. His mustache was hanging off his face, and his hat was crushed under a shoulder.

"Nothing but a fancy pile of rags," Steele said to the body. "That's all you ever were."

He holstered his pistol, when the bartender said, "Lawrence hollered you robbed him." He pulled a shotgun from under the bar. "I think you got some questions to answer, fella."

"We never robbed anybody," Steele replied. "That was just a ruse, a reason to fire at us first." He nodded toward a distant cluster of buildings. "That Fort Laramie?"

The bartender nodded.

"Let me bring the military in on this. Maybe they didn't know about Lawrence and Clark here, but they can find out and clear us."

"Looky that mustache," came a voice. "That guy was a phony."

There were mutters of agreement.

"Good enough," said the bartender. "We'll get the Army in on this."

"Meanwhile, this man needs a doctor," Elizabeth pointed to Steele's bleeding arm.

"There's one up the street."

The two heard several other unfavorable remarks about Clark and Lawrence as they were leaving.

"I take it those two were not popular here, either," Steele said.

"Scum makes its own dirty water," said Elizabeth. Then she looked puzzled. "Did I say that right?"

"I don't know," Steele said, "but we both know what you mean."

And, in spite of avenging the death of Elizabeth's father, Steele's bleeding wound, in spite of the time it would for the military to clear them, Steele and Elizabeth looked at each other and saw love and humor and good things ahead.

They smiled, and held each other's hands, heading for a bright future—and the doctor's office.